THE PELICAN SHAKESPEARE

GENERAL EDITOR ALFRED HARBAGE

TWELFTH NIGHT

WILLIAM SHAKESPEARE

TWELFTH NIGHT

OR

WHAT YOU WILL

EDITED BY CHARLES T. PROUTY

PENGUIN BOOKS

Penguin Books
625 Madison Avenue
New York, New York 10022

First published in *The Pelican Shakespeare* 1958
This revised edition first published 1972
Reprinted 1974, 1978

Copyright © Penguin Books, Inc., 1958, 1972
All rights reserved

Library of Congress catalog card number: 79-98357

Printed in the United States of America by
Kingsport Press, Inc., Kingsport, Tennessee
Set in Monotype Ehrhardt and Linotype Times Roman

CONTENTS

PUBLISHER'S NOTE

Soon after the thirty-eight volumes forming *The Pelican Shakespeare* had been published, they were brought together in *The Complete Pelican Shakespeare*. The editorial revisions and new textual features are explained in detail in the General Editor's Preface to the one-volume edition. They have all been incorporated in the present volume. The following should be mentioned in particular:

The lines are not numbered in arbitrary units. Instead all lines are numbered which contain a word, phrase, or allusion explained in the glossarial notes. In the occasional instances where there is a long stretch of unannotated text, certain lines are numbered in italics to serve the conventional reference purpose.

The intrusive and often inaccurate place-headings inserted by early editors are omitted (as is becoming standard practise), but for the convenience of those who miss them, an indication of locale now appears as first item in the annotation of each scene.

In the interest of both elegance and utility, each speech-prefix is set in a separate line when the speaker's lines are in verse, except when these words form the second half of a pentameter line. Thus the verse form of the speech is kept visually intact, and turned-over lines are avoided. What is printed as verse and what is printed as prose has, in general, the authority of the original texts. Departures from the original texts in this regard have only the authority of editorial tradition and the judgment of the Pelican editors; and, in a few instances, are admittedly arbitrary.

SHAKESPEARE AND
HIS STAGE

William Shakespeare was christened in Holy Trinity Church, Stratford-upon-Avon, April 26, 1564. His birth is traditionally assigned to April 23. He was the eldest of four boys and two girls who survived infancy in the family of John Shakespeare, glover and trader of Henley Street, and his wife Mary Arden, daughter of a small landowner of Wilmcote. In 1568 John was elected Bailiff (equivalent to Mayor) of Stratford, having already filled the minor municipal offices. The town maintained for the sons of the burgesses a free school, taught by a university graduate and offering preparation in Latin sufficient for university entrance; its early registers are lost, but there can be little doubt that Shakespeare received the formal part of his education in this school.

On November 27, 1582, a license was issued for the marriage of William Shakespeare (aged eighteen) and Ann Hathaway (aged twenty-six), and on May 26, 1583, their child Susanna was christened in Holy Trinity Church. The inference that the marriage was forced upon the youth is natural but not inevitable; betrothal was legally binding at the time, and was sometimes regarded as conferring conjugal rights. Two additional children of the marriage, the twins Hamnet and Judith, were christened on February 2, 1585. Meanwhile the prosperity of the elder Shakespeares had declined, and William was impelled to seek a career outside Stratford.

The tradition that he spent some time as a country

teacher is old but unverifiable. Because of the absence of records his early twenties are called the "lost years," and only one thing about them is certain – that at least some of these years were spent in winning a place in the acting profession. He may have begun as a provincial trouper, but by 1592 he was established in London and prominent enough to be attacked. In a pamphlet of that year, *Groats-worth of Wit*, the ailing Robert Greene complained of the neglect which university writers like himself had suffered from actors, one of whom was daring to set up as a playwright:

. . . an vpstart Crow, beautified with our feathers, that with his *Tygers hart wrapt in a Players hyde*, supposes he is as well able to bombast out a blanke verse as the best of you: and beeing an absolute *Iohannes fac totum*, is in his owne conceit the onely Shake-scene in a countrey.

The pun on his name, and the parody of his line "O tiger's heart wrapped in a woman's hide" (*3 Henry VI*), pointed clearly to Shakespeare. Some of his admirers protested, and Henry Chettle, the editor of Greene's pamphlet, saw fit to apologize:

. . . I am as sory as if the originall fault had beene my fault, because my selfe haue seene his demeanor no lesse ciuill than he excelent in the qualitie he professes : Besides, diuers of worship haue reported his vprightnes of dealing, which argues his honesty, and his facetious grace in writting, that approoues his Art. (Prefatory epistle, *Kind-Harts Dreame*)

The plague closed the London theatres for many months in 1592–94, denying the actors their livelihood. To this period belong Shakespeare's two narrative poems, *Venus and Adonis* and *The Rape of Lucrece*, both dedicated to the Earl of Southampton. No doubt the poet was rewarded with a gift of money as usual in such cases, but he did no further dedicating and we have no reliable information on whether Southampton, or anyone else, became his regular patron. His sonnets, first mentioned in 1598 and published without his consent in 1609, are intimate without being explicitly autobiographical. They seem to commemorate the poet's friendship with an idealized youth, rivalry with a more favored poet, and love affair with a dark mistress; and his bitterness when the mistress betrays him in conjunction with the friend; but it is difficult to decide precisely what the "story" is, impossible to decide whether it is fictional or true. The true distinction of the sonnets, at least of those not purely conventional, rests in the universality of the thoughts and moods they express, and in their poignancy and beauty.

In 1594 was formed the theatrical company known until 1603 as the Lord Chamberlain's men, thereafter as the King's men. Its original membership included, besides Shakespeare, the beloved clown Will Kempe and the famous actor Richard Burbage. The company acted in various London theatres and even toured the provinces, but it is chiefly associated in our minds with the Globe Theatre built on the south bank of the Thames in 1599. Shakespeare was an actor and joint owner of this company (and its Globe) through the remainder of his creative years. His plays, written at the average rate of two a year, together with Burbage's acting won it its place of leadership among the London companies.

Individual plays began to appear in print, in editions both honest and piratical, and the publishers became increasingly aware of the value of Shakespeare's name on the title pages. As early as 1598 he was hailed as the leading English dramatist in the *Palladis Tamia* of Francis Meres:

As *Plautus* and *Seneca* are accounted the best for Comedy and Tragedy among the Latines, so *Shakespeare* among the English is the most excellent in both kinds for the stage: for Comedy, witnes his *Gentlemen of Verona*, his *Errors*, his *Loue labors lost*, his *Loue labours wonne* [at one time in print but no longer extant, at least under this title], his *Midsummers night dream*, & his *Merchant of Venice*; for Tragedy, his *Richard the 2*, *Richard the 3*, *Henry the 4*, *King Iohn*, *Titus Andronicus*, and his *Romeo and Iuliet*.

The note is valuable both in indicating Shakespeare's pres-
tige and in helping us to establish a chronology. In the
second half of his writing career, history plays gave place
to the great tragedies; and farces and light comedies gave
place to the problem plays and symbolic romances. In
1623, seven years after his death, his former fellow-actors,
John Heminge and Henry Condell, cooperated with a
group of London printers in bringing out his plays in col-
lected form. The volume is generally known as the First
Folio.

Shakespeare had never severed his relations with Stratford. His wife and children may sometimes have shared
his London lodgings, but their home was Stratford. His
son Hamnet was buried there in 1596, and his daughters
Susanna and Judith were married there in 1607 and 1616
respectively. (His father, for whom he had secured a coat
of arms and thus the privilege of writing himself gentleman, died in 1601, his mother in 1608.) His considerable
earnings in London, as actor-sharer, part owner of the
Globe, and playwright, were invested chiefly in Stratford
property. In 1597 he purchased for £60 New Place, one of
the two most imposing residences in the town. A number
of other business transactions, as well as minor episodes in
his career, have left documentary records. By 1611 he was
in a position to retire, and he seems gradually to have
withdrawn from theatrical activity in order to live in
Stratford. In March, 1616, he made a will, leaving token
bequests to Burbage, Heminge, and Condell, but the bulk
of his estate to his family. The most famous feature of the
will, the bequest of the second-best bed to his wife, reveals
nothing about Shakespeare's marriage; the quaintness of
the provision seems commonplace to those familiar with
ancient testaments. Shakespeare died April 23, 1616, and
was buried in the Stratford church where he had been
christened. Within seven years a monument was erected
to his memory on the north wall of the chancel. Its portrait bust and the Droeshout engraving on the title page of

the First Folio provide the only likenesses with an established claim to authenticity. The best verbal vignette was written by his rival Ben Jonson, the more impressive for being imbedded in a context mainly critical:

... I loved the man, and doe honour his memory (on this side idolatry) as much as any. Hee was indeed honest, and of an open and free nature: had an excellent Phantsie, brave notions, and gentle expressions.... (*Timber or Discoveries*, ca. 1623–30)

*

The reader of Shakespeare's plays is aided by a general knowledge of the way in which they were staged. The King's men acquired a roofed and artificially lighted theatre only toward the close of Shakespeare's career, and then only for winter use. Nearly all his plays were designed for performance in such structures as the Globe – a three-tiered amphitheatre with a large rectangular platform extending to the center of its yard. The plays were staged by daylight, by large casts brilliantly costumed, but with only a minimum of properties, without scenery, and quite possibly without intermissions. There was a rear stage gallery for action "above," and a curtained rear recess for "discoveries" and other special effects, but by far the major portion of any play was enacted upon the projecting platform, with episode following episode in swift succession, and with shifts of time and place signaled the audience only by the momentary clearing of the stage between the episodes. Information about the identity of the characters and, when necessary, about the time and place of the action was incorporated in the dialogue. No place-headings have been inserted in the present editions; these are apt to obscure the original fluidity of structure, with the emphasis upon action and speech rather than scenic background. (Indications of place are supplied in the footnotes.) The acting, including that of the youthful apprentices to the profession who performed the parts of women, was highly skillful, with a premium placed upon grace of gesture and beauty of diction. The audiences, a cross section of the general public, commonly numbered a thousand, sometimes more than two thousand. Judged by the type of plays they applauded, these audiences were not only large but also perceptive.

THE TEXTS OF THE PLAYS

About half of Shakespeare's plays appeared in print for the first time in the folio volume of 1623. The others had been published individually, usually in quarto volumes, during his lifetime or in the six years following his death. The copy used by the printers of the quartos varied greatly in merit, sometimes representing Shakespeare's true text, sometimes only a debased version of that text. The copy used by the printers of the folio also varied in merit, but was chosen with care. Since it consisted of the best available manuscripts, or the more acceptable quartos (although frequently in editions other than the first), or of quartos corrected by reference to manuscripts, we have good or reasonably good texts of most of the thirty-seven plays.

In the present series, the plays have been newly edited from quarto or folio texts, depending, when a choice offered, upon which is now regarded by bibliographical specialists as the more authoritative. The ideal has been to reproduce the chosen texts with as few alterations as possible, beyond occasional relineation, expansion of abbreviations, and modernization of punctuation and spelling. Emendation is held to a minimum, and such material as has been added, in the way of stage directions and lines supplied by an alternative text, has been enclosed in square brackets.

None of the plays printed in Shakespeare's lifetime were divided into acts and scenes, and the inference is that the author's own manuscripts were not so divided. In the folio collection, some of the plays remained undivided, some were divided into acts, and some were divided into acts and scenes. During the eighteenth century all of the plays were divided into acts and scenes, and in the Cambridge edition of the mid-nineteenth century, from which the influential Globe text derived, this division was more or less regularized and the lines were numbered. Many useful works of reference employ the act–scene–line apparatus thus established.

Since this act–scene division is obviously convenient, but is of very dubious authority so far as Shakespeare's own structural principles are concerned, or the original manner of staging his plays, a problem is presented to modern editors. In the present series the act–scene division is retained marginally, and may be viewed as a reference aid like the line numbering. A star marks the points of division when these points have been determined by a cleared stage indicating a shift of time and place in the action of the play, or when no harm results from the editorial assumption that there is such a shift. However, at those points where the established division is clearly misleading – that is, where continuous action has been split up into separate "scenes" – the star is omitted and the distortion corrected. This mechanical expedient seemed the best means of combining utility and accuracy.

THE GENERAL EDITOR

INTRODUCTION

On Candlemas Day, 1602, the Gentlemen of the Middle Temple, one of the Inns of Court, held their feast, and for their entertainment there was performed "... a play called 'Twelue Night, or What You Will' . . . ." John Manningham, a spectator on this occasion, continues his account with a description of the play, which was

... much like the Commedy of Errores, or Menechmi in Plautus, but most like and neere to that in Italian called *Inganni*. A good practise in it to make the Steward beleeve his Lady widdowe was in love with him, by counterfeyting a letter as from his Lady in generall termes, telling him what shee liked best in him, and prescribing his gesture in smiling, his apparaile, &c., and then when he came to practise making him beleeue they tooke him to be mad.

Since other evidence suggests that *Twelfth Night* may have been written as early as 1599, we may safely date it "about 1600." Whether it was written before *As You Like It* or *Much Ado about Nothing*, both certainly in existence by 1600, cannot be determined exactly. Actually all three of these "Joyous Comedies" are thematically of a piece, and any precise ordering of their composition can only be based on subjective judgments. In some ways it is tempting to accept Dr Leslie Hotson's recent theory that *Twelfth Night* was first performed on January 6, 1601, before the Queen at Whitehall with Don Virginio Orsino as an honored guest. There are, however, several objections to this theory and we must still rely on the approximate date of 1600. That the visiting Italian nobleman would have been flattered by the character of the Duke Orsino is somewhat difficult to understand.

In contrast to *As You Like It,* which has a single source, the sources or analogues of *Twelfth Night* are manifold. Manningham refers to two possible sources, Plautus' *Menaechmi* and the Italian *Inganni.* Modern scholarship has added to the list another Italian play *Gl'Ingannati* (which has characters named Fabio and Malevolti as well as a reference to Epiphany, or Twelfth Night), Italian *novelle,* French and English translations of the latter, Sidney's *Arcadia,* the play of *Sir Clyomon and Clamydes,* and Emanuel Forde's *Parismus* (which has the shipwreck as well as the names Olivia and Violetta). These deal in varying fashion with twins and the disguise of the girl as a page wooing in her master's behalf. As a matter of fact, Shakespeare had already used this latter device in *The Two Gentlemen of Verona* with the disguised Julia in the service of her false lover Proteus.

In all these varied materials there is no suggestion of the Malvolio plot, but a possible clue as to why Shakespeare added this to the traditional materials may be found in one of the English sources, the tale of Apolonius and Silla, as related by Barnabe Riche in a collection entitled *Riche his Farewell to Militarie Profession.* The reason for this rather odd title is that Riche, abandoning the wars, now prepares to devote his labors "for the onely delight of the courteous Gentlewomen bothe of England and Irelande." The story itself is remote from Shakespeare's play in many respects. Duke Apolonius, returning from war against the Turks, is forced by a storm to take refuge in Cyprus. Silla, daughter of Pontus the governor of the island, promptly falls in love with the noble visitor. After his departure for Constantinople, she sets off in pursuit accompanied by a faithful servant. After a shipwreck, Silla disguises herself and gains service as a page to Apolonius, and must then woo, on his behalf, the Lady Julina. Silla's twin brother Silvio arrives in search of his sister and is mistaken for her by Julina. Complications ensue when the impetuous Julina becomes pregnant by Silvio without benefit of wedlock. Silvio has departed in further search for his sister, but fortunately returns in time to marry Julina, while Silla wins her Apolonius.

What is more interesting to us than the story itself is the prefatory comment of Riche on the subject of love and its particular manifestations in the tale. The conventions of love were of great concern to the young ladies and gentlemen of the Queen's Court and they were aped by those beneath them in the social scale. And it is these conventions, social and literary, that Shakespeare views with Puck's amused observation – Lord, what fools these mortals be! – in all three of the Joyous Comedies. Riche, however, sees no humor in his story, as his words witness:

There is no child that is borne into this wretched worlde, but before it doeth sucke the mother's milke, it taketh first a soope of the cupp of errour, which maketh us, when we come to riper yeres, not onely to enter into actions of injurie, but many tymes to straie from that is right and reason; but in all other thinges, wherein wee shewe our selves to bee moste dronken with this poisoned cuppe, it is in our actions of love; for the lover is so estranged from that is right, and wandereth so wide from the boundes of reason, that he is not able to deeme white from blacke, good from badde, vertue from vice; but onely led by the apetite of his owne affections, and groundyng them on the foolishnesse of his owne fancies, will so settle his likyng on such a one, as either by desert or unworthinesse will merite rather to be loathed then loved.

The unreasoning choice of lovers is exemplified in the story at hand, as Riche states:

Wherfore, right curteous gentilwomen, if it please you with pacience to persue this historie following, you shall see Dame Errour so plaie her parte with a leishe of lovers, a male and twoo femalles, as shall woorke a wonder to your wise judgement, in notyng the effecte of their amorous devises and conclusions of their actions : the firste neclectyng the love of a noble dame, yong, beautifull, and faire, who onely for his good will plaied the parte of a serving manne, contented to abide any maner of paine onely to behold him : he again setting his love of a dame, that despysing hym (beeyng a noble Duke) gave her self to a servyng manne (as she had thought); but it otherwise fell out, as the substance of this tale shall better discribe.

Just what group of "curteous gentilwomen" Riche was addressing is a question. In his attitude toward love and lovers he is not following the courtly or Petrarchan tradition with its glorification of love and its absorbed interest in the subtleties of the conventions. Instead Riche, in 1581, is speaking with the harsh moralistic voice of the emerging bourgeois Puritan. In 1567 Geoffrey Fenton had translated a number of tales from the French of Belleforest with the avowed object of praising virtuous love and excoriating vice, thus hoping that "the younglings of our countrey in reding my indevor, maye break the slepe of their longe follye, and retire at last to amendement of lyfe." For Fenton, as for his French source, and for Riche, love was a disease which deprived man or woman of reason. This idea was not original with these particular authors; it had wide currency particularly in the middle class and may be traced to the classic past in Ovid's *De Remediis Amoris*, wherein that poet discusses remedies for the disease of love.

From this all-too-brief treatment of a large and complicated problem, it becomes clear that Riche and Shakespeare regard the story of the "leishe of lovers" from quite different points of view. Riche's use of "leishe" (leash), borrowed from the terminology of hunting and meaning a set of three hounds bound together, is sufficiently indicative of his moral scorn. For Riche the absolute folly and utter lack of rational conduct caused by love is demonstrated by the shifts which occur. Apolonius loves Julina; Julina loves the disguised Silla, who in turn loves Apolonius. At the end Apolonius marries Silla, and Julina the twin brother Silvio. Love that changes so rapidly and with so little motivation is unreasoning and senseless.

But out of this very shift in the affections Shakespeare has created the gay and charming world of Illyria. His theme is love but there the similarity with Riche ends, for Shakespeare is not interested in moral judgments; he accepts the conventions of love as they existed in the courtly world. Of course people fall in love at first sight; they always do in the love poems and romances of the age. Orsino, Viola, and Olivia all behave in thoroughly traditional fashion. In his opening scene (I, i, 20–24) Orsino describes his fall:

> O, when mine eyes did see Olivia first,
> Methought she purged the air of pestilence.
> That instant was I turned into a hart,
> And my desires, like fell and cruel hounds,
> E'er since pursue me.

Whereas we have had some indication that the noble Duke suffers from love's torments, we are quite unprepared, at least by any dialogue, for Viola's sudden fall. Ordered by Orsino to woo Olivia on his behalf, Viola acquiesces (I, iv, 39–41):

> I'll do my best
> To woo your lady. [aside] Yet a barful strife!
> Whoe'er I woo, myself would be his wife.

Olivia requires a few more lines than Viola to announce her capitulation, but she is well aware of the rapidity of the fall (I, v, 278–84).

Thy tongue, thy face, thy limbs, actions, and spirit
Do give thee fivefold blazon. Not too fast; soft, soft,
Unless the master were the man. How now?
Even so quickly may one catch the plague?
Methinks I feel this youth's perfections
With an invisible and subtle stealth
To creep in at mine eyes. Well, let it be.

The nature of the love which afflicts our characters is
not oversubtly revealed. The sophisticated Duke, well
read in love's literature, needs but one cue to pun and
learnedly compare. Concluding his apostrophe to the
spirit of love, he is asked a simple question by Curio, "Will
you go hunt, my lord?" but his seemingly simple re-
sponse is well pointed in the proper direction, "What,
Curio?" The answer is the one he wants, "The hart."
Immediately Olivia becomes the hart (heart), "Why, so I
do, the noblest that I have," which he pursues. At the
next moment we are plunged into Ovid's *Metamorphoses*
when the Duke now compares himself, after he has first
seen Olivia, with Actaeon, who, having gazed on the nude
Diana bathing, was punished by being transformed into a
hart and pursued to death by his own hounds. Such
mental agility, such appropriate references turned to the
occasion of the moment were the very essence of the true
courtly lover. Orsino knows the game, but Shakespeare
has made him play it in seriousness.

In contrast, Olivia calmly accepts her infection with
love's plague by the simple line, "Well, let it be." But this
is deceptive simplicity, for properly read by a skilled
actress this can be a most trenchant instance of high
comedy travelling in an instant from all the conventional
pretensions of her preceding lines to an amused reality.

Just such a tone distinguishes the difference in the
various attitudes toward love found, for example, in I, v,
where Viola goes a-wooing for Orsino. Here, particularly
after the departure of Maria, when the two women are

alone, we see that both are well skilled in the dialectic of love. Olivia opens with a well-known gambit, "Now, sir, what is your text?" This is the familiar association of love as a religion with its holy books, and the two play through "what chapter" to "heresy." The point of this and the subsequent dialogue is that each knows that the other is playing the game, so that this knowledge on the part of the aware spectator develops the comic value, not so much of ridicule, as amused observation of the game itself. These two can see themselves objectively but Orsino cannot, nor can Malvolio.

In the source materials of the main plot, it would seem that Shakespeare saw the elements of high comedy. Here in a traditional story that had been told many times, always seriously, was an example of the absurdity of the literary conventions of love. As we have seen, it is with an amused eye that he views this story. At the first we have Orsino luxuriating in his own emotions; he is more in love with love than with Olivia. His opening soliloquy is too much of a good thing and would have been so recognized by a cultivated Elizabethan. This delineation of Orsino is amplified as the play progresses: in II, iv, he describes himself as a true lover, ringing the changes on the clichés; in Act V he epitomizes the eternal vacillations and improbabilities when at one moment he is prepared to kill Viola and in the next to marry her.

Similarly Olivia, having fallen in love with the disguised Viola, is perfectly willing to marry the twin brother Sebastian. If comment were needed on this sudden shift, we need only look back to Viola's analysis of the situation in II, ii. Olivia has sent Malvolio in pursuit of Viola-Cesario with a love ring, and the latter immediately recognizes what has happened:

I left no ring with her. What means this lady?
Fortune forbid my outside have not charmed her.

It is precisely with the outside, external aspects of the formalized love conventions that the main plot deals and therein lies another aspect of the humor. Nothing is serious, and after all the subtitle of the play is "What You Will."

On the other hand the subplot does approach the serious when Malvolio is imprisoned as a lunatic. Some critics have, in fact, said that Malvolio is dealt with much too harshly. It is precisely on this point that we may observe Shakespeare's probable reason for adding the characters and incidents of this original plot to a well-known story. Love is the controlling factor in both plots but here we have a quite different set of lovers. Aguecheek is urged on by Sir Toby to think that he may win Olivia. Malvolio, tricked by the letter, but led on by his own self-love, fancies himself as suitor and husband to Olivia. In the final resolution of Act V we hear from Fabian that Sir Toby has married Maria in recompense for her writing of the letter. Now the world in which these characters function is quite different from that of Orsino, Viola, and Olivia.

Sir Andrew is a mere caricature of the traditional lover, and this is pointed by the direct contrast between Sir Toby's description of him and the actuality which we see on his entrance a few lines later on. These are the attributes given him by Sir Toby: "as tall a man as any's in Illyria" ("tall" here means "brave," "outstanding"); "he plays o' th' viol-de-gamboys, and speaks three or four languages word for word without book, and hath all the good gifts of nature." If true, this description would well suit a gentleman seeking to follow the ideal of *The Courtier*. But Sir Andrew is, as Maria says, a "fool and a prodigal." Further he is stupid and vain, as his lines disclose when he completely misunderstands Sir Toby's injunction, "Accost, Sir Andrew, accost." He specifically points out his lack of knowledge of foreign languages, and though

priding himself on his skill in dancing and in fencing he is
last seen in I, iii, cutting a ludicrous caper, while subse-
quently both he and Sir Toby are given a sound beating in
a fencing bout with Sebastian.

Equally apart from the tradition is Malvolio, who is
early charged by Olivia with being "sick of self-love" and
lacking a "free disposition." Through self-love he can
naturally assume that the letter is meant for him and that
it was written by the Lady Olivia. Even before he has
found the letter in II, v, he is dreaming of such a marriage,
but love for Malvolio has but one aspect: his own aggran-
dizement. He will become "Count Malvolio," will wear
"some rich jewel," and Sir Toby will curtsy to him. To
achieve such position and wealth he will, of course, wear
yellow stockings and be ever cross-gartered. He will even
attempt a free disposition and will smile.

Here then are two who have truly fallen into error, but
it is not as a result of love. The fault lies rather in their own
characters and attitudes toward love. Sir Andrew is fool
enough to think himself a proper lover, and for his pains
loses his money to Sir Toby and gets a good beating. Malvolio is presumptuous enough to think first of all that his
lady would favor him and secondly that he could rise from
his position as steward to that of lord of the household.
Finally Sir Toby marries almost by inadvertence.

Thus the subplot may be seen as representing the ob-
verse, the other side of the coin. In the main plot the
characters move in the world of an established convention
while in the other the characters are alien, if not anti-
thetical, to the convention. We can smile with Olivia as
she accepts love with "Well, let it be," or with Viola as
she realizes that Olivia has fallen in love with her disguise:

> O Time, thou must untangle this, not I;
> It is too hard a knot for me t' untie.

In direct contrast with this spirit of high comedy we have
the plots and trickery of low comedy where we laugh at

Sir Andrew, Malvolio, and even Sir Toby, whose gulling of Sir Andrew into a duel has brought him "a bloody cox-comb." Two worlds of love and two worlds of comedy have been fused into *Twelfth Night, or, What You Will.*

The conventions and pretenses are not mocked in the satiric spirit, for here all is gaiety, and the lyricism which animates the play is found not only in the songs but in the characters themselves. When Viola describes how she would woo were she in love (I, v, 254–62), or tells Orsino of her concealed love (II, iv, 109–17), her lines sing with the ideal quality that is hers. So too both Orsino and Olivia reveal that they belong to the world of fancy or, in Sir Toby's words, a land of "cakes and ale" far removed from the mundane. Feste sums it all in his concluding stanza:

> A great while ago the world begun,
>   With hey, ho, the wind and the rain;
> But that's all one, our play is done,
>   And we'll strive to please you every day.

Yale University   CHARLES T. PROUTY

NOTE ON THE TEXT

The only text for *Twelfth Night* is that of the folio, which appears to have been printed from the prompt-copy or possibly a transcript of it. It is an excellent text, and it is here followed closely. There is some evidence that the text contains revisions of the copy originally designed for performance. In the second scene Viola says that she will enter Orsino's service as his eunuch (that is, his singer) and will "speak to him in many sorts of music," but in II, iv, when Viola-Cesario is asked by Orsino to sing, she does not do so; instead Feste is sent for. Evidently the boy playing the part of Viola was not deemed an adequate singer, so that additional dialogue was written to get Feste on the stage. (There is also a possibility that Malvolio's lines at II, v, 36–37, are an interpolation, since they may refer to an event of 1616.) The act–scene division supplied marginally is identical with that of the folio.

23

Following is a complete list of substantive departures from the
folio text, with the adopted reading in italics followed by the folio
reading in roman.

I, ii, 15 *Arion* Orion

I, iii, 48 *Andrew* Ma.   50 *Mary Accost* Mary, accost   55 *Fare*
Far   82 *Pourquoi* Pur-quoy   83 *pourquoi* purquoy   89 *curl
by* coole my   90 *me* we   92 *housewife* huswife   114 *Mall's*
Mals   122 *dun* dam'd   *set* sit   125 *That's* That

I, iv, 27 *nuncio's* Nuntio's

I, v, 109 *comes* – comes   141 *Has* Ha's   159 s.d. *Viola* Violenta
162 *beauty* – beautie.   199 *olive* Olyffe   241 *with fertile* fertill

II, ii, 11 *me.* me,   19 *as methought* methought   30 *our* O   31
made of, such made, if such

II, iii, 2 *diluculo* Deliculo   24 *leman* Lemon   31 *a–* a   124 *a
nayword* an ayword

II, iv, 52 *Fly . . . fly* fye . . . fie   87 *I* It   98 *suffers* suffer

II, v, 57 *my* – *some* my some   106 *staniel* stallion   120 *sequel.
That* sequell that   133 *born* become   *achieve* atcheeues   146–
47 *Unhappy.' Daylight* vnhappy daylight   163 *dear* deero

III, i, 8 *king lies* King s lyes   66 *wise men, folly-fall'n* wisemens
folly falne   69 *vous garde* vou garde   70 *vous aussi; votre*
vouz ousie vostre   88 *all ready* already

III, ii, 7 *thee the* the

III, iv, 22 *Olivia* Mal.   64 *tang* langer   82 *How . . . man* (joined
to preceding speech by Fabian in F)   155 *Fare thee well* Far-
theewell   161 *You* Yon   231 *competent* Computent   242 s.d.
Exit Exit Toby   335 *babbling, drunkenness* babling drunken-
nesse   374 s.d. *Exeunt* Exit

IV, ii, 5 *in* in in   37 *clerestories* cleere stores   69 *sport to* sport

V, i, 112 *thief* thief,   192 *pavin* panym   198 *help? An* help an
339 *mad. Thou cam'st* mad ; then cam'st   383, 387, 391, 395 *the
wind . . . rain* &c.   385, 389, 393 *it . . . day* &c.   395 *With hey*
hey

TWELFTH NIGHT
OR
WHAT YOU WILL

[NAMES OF THE ACTORS

Orsino, Duke of Illyria
Sebastian, brother of Viola
Antonio, a sea captain, friend to Sebastian
A Sea Captain, friend to Viola
Valentine
Curio } *gentlemen attending on the Duke*
Sir Toby Belch, uncle to Olivia
Sir Andrew Aguecheek
Malvolio, steward to Olivia
Fabian
Feste, a clown } *servants to Olivia*
Olivia, a countess
Viola, sister of Sebastian
Maria, Olivia's woman
Lords, a Priest, Sailors, Officers, Musicians,
  and Attendants

Scene : *Illyria*]

TWELFTH NIGHT

OR

WHAT YOU WILL

Enter Orsino Duke of Illyria, Curio, and other Lords　I, i
[with Musicians].

DUKE
 If music be the food of love, play on,
 Give me excess of it, that, surfeiting,
 The appetite may sicken, and so die.
 That strain again. It had a dying fall;　　　　　　　4
 O, it came o'er my ear like the sweet sound
 That breathes upon a bank of violets,
 Stealing and giving odor. Enough, no more.
 'Tis not so sweet now as it was before.
 O spirit of love, how quick and fresh art thou,　　9
 That, notwithstanding thy capacity,
 Receiveth as the sea. Nought enters there,
 Of what validity and pitch soe'er,　　　　　　　　12
 But falls into abatement and low price
 Even in a minute. So full of shapes is fancy　　14
 That it alone is high fantastical.　　　　　　　　15
CURIO
 Will you go hunt, my lord?
DUKE
 What, Curio?
CURIO
 The hart.

I, i The palace of Duke Orsino　　4 *fall* cadence　　9 *quick* alive　　12 *validity*
value; *pitch* i.e. worth (in falconry, high point of a falcon's flight)　　14 *shapes*
imagined forms; *fancy* love　　15 *high fantastical* highly imaginative

DUKE
Why, so I do, the noblest that I have.
O, when mine eyes did see Olivia first,
Methought she purged the air of pestilence.
22   That instant was I turned into a hart,
23   And my desires, like fell and cruel hounds,
E'er since pursue me.
      Enter Valentine.
                 How now? What news from her?

VALENTINE
So please my lord, I might not be admitted;
But from her handmaid do return this answer:
27   The element itself, till seven years' heat,
Shall not behold her face at ample view;
But like a cloistress she will veilèd walk,
And water once a day her chamber round
31   With eye-offending brine: all this to season
A brother's dead love, which she would keep fresh
And lasting in her sad remembrance.

DUKE
O, she that hath a heart of that fine frame
To pay this debt of love but to a brother,
36   How will she love when the rich golden shaft
Hath killed the flock of all affections else
That live in her; when liver, brain, and heart,
These sovereign thrones, are all supplied and filled,
Her sweet perfections, with one self king.
Away before me to sweet beds of flow'rs;
Love-thoughts lie rich when canopied with bow'rs.
                         Exeunt.

*

22–24 *hart . . . me* (alluding to the story of Actaeon, turned into a hart by Diana and killed by his own hounds)   **23** *fell* savage   **27** *element* sky; *heat* course   **31** *season* preserve   **36–37** *when . . . else* i.e. when Cupid's arrow has slain all emotions except love

Enter Viola, a Captain, and Sailors.   I, ii

VIOLA
What country, friends, is this?

CAPTAIN
This is Illyria, lady.   2

VIOLA
And what should I do in Illyria?
My brother he is in Elysium.   4
Perchance he is not drowned. What think you, sailors?

CAPTAIN
It is perchance that you yourself were saved.

VIOLA
O my poor brother, and so perchance may he be.

CAPTAIN
True, madam; and, to comfort you with chance,   8
Assure yourself, after our ship did split,
When you, and those poor number saved with you,
Hung on our driving boat, I saw your brother,   11
Most provident in peril, bind himself
(Courage and hope both teaching him the practice)
To a strong mast that lived upon the sea;   14
Where, like Arion on the dolphin's back,   15
I saw him hold acquaintance with the waves
So long as I could see.

VIOLA
For saying so, there's gold.
Mine own escape unfoldeth to my hope,   19
Whereto thy speech serves for authority
The like of him. Know'st thou this country?

CAPTAIN
Ay, madam, well, for I was bred and born
Not three hours' travel from this very place.

I, ii The seacoast of Illyria 2 *Illyria* on the east coast of the Adriatic
4 *Elysium* home of the blessed dead 8 *chance* what may have happened
11 *driving* drifting 14 *lived* floated 15 *Arion* a Greek bard who leapt
overboard to escape murderous sailors, and charmed dolphins with the
music of his lyre so that they bore him to land 19 *unfoldeth to my hope* gives
me hope (for my brother)

VIOLA
Who governs here?

CAPTAIN
A noble duke, in nature as in name.

VIOLA
What is his name?

CAPTAIN
Orsino.

VIOLA
Orsino! I have heard my father name him.
He was a bachelor then.

CAPTAIN
And so is now, or was so very late;
For but a month ago I went from hence,
32   And then 'twas fresh in murmur (as you know
What great ones do, the less will prattle of)
That he did seek the love of fair Olivia.

VIOLA
What's she?

CAPTAIN
A virtuous maid, the daughter of a count
That died some twelvemonth since, then leaving her
In the protection of his son, her brother,
Who shortly also died; for whose dear love,
They say, she hath abjured the sight
And company of men.

VIOLA   O that I served that lady,
42   And might not be delivered to the world,
43   Till I had made mine own occasion mellow,
44   What my estate is.

CAPTAIN   That were hard to compass,
Because she will admit no kind of suit,
No, not the Duke's.

---

32 *fresh in murmur* a current rumor   42 *delivered* revealed   43 *mellow* ready
to be revealed   44 *estate* position in society

VIOLA

There is a fair behavior in thee, captain,   47
And though that nature with a beauteous wall
Doth oft close in pollution, yet of thee
I will believe thou hast a mind that suits
With this thy fair and outward character.   51
I prithee (and I'll pay thee bounteously)
Conceal me what I am, and be my aid
For such disguise as haply shall become
The form of my intent. I'll serve this duke.   55
Thou shalt present me as an eunuch to him;   56
It may be worth thy pains. For I can sing,
And speak to him in many sorts of music
That will allow me very worth his service.   59
What else may hap, to time I will commit;
Only shape thou thy silence to my wit.

CAPTAIN

Be you his eunuch, and your mute I'll be;
When my tongue blabs, then let mine eyes not see.

VIOLA

I thank thee. Lead me on.   *Exeunt.*

*

Enter Sir Toby and Maria.   I, iii

TOBY What a plague means my niece to take the death of
her brother thus? I am sure care's an enemy to life.

MARIA By my troth, Sir Toby, you must come in earlier
o' nights. Your cousin, my lady, takes great exceptions   4
to your ill hours.

TOBY Why, let her except before excepted.   6

47 *behavior* both 'conduct' and 'appearance'   51 *character* personal
appearance indicating moral qualities   55 *form of my intent* my outward
purpose   56 *eunuch* i.e. singer (but she enters his service simply as a page)
59 *allow me* cause me to be considered
l, iii The house of Countess Olivia   4 *cousin* kinsman   6 *except before
excepted* (cant legal phrase)

MARIA Ay, but you must confine yourself within the modest limits of order.

9 TOBY Confine? I'll confine myself no finer than I am. These clothes are good enough to drink in, and so be

11 these boots too. An they be not, let them hang themselves in their own straps.

MARIA That quaffing and drinking will undo you. I heard my lady talk of it yesterday; and of a foolish knight that you brought in one night here to be her wooer.

TOBY Who? Sir Andrew Aguecheek?

MARIA Ay, he.

18 TOBY He's as tall a man as any's in Illyria.

MARIA What's that to th' purpose?

TOBY Why, he has three thousand ducats a year.

MARIA Ay, but he'll have but a year in all these ducats. He's a very fool and a prodigal.

23 TOBY Fie that you'll say so! He plays o' th' viol-de-gamboys, and speaks three or four languages word for word

25 without book, and hath all the good gifts of nature.

26 MARIA He hath, indeed, almost natural; for, besides that he's a fool, he's a great quarreller; and but that he hath

28 the gift of a coward to allay the gust he hath in quarrelling, 'tis thought among the prudent he would quickly have the gift of a grave.

31 TOBY By this hand, they are scoundrels and substractors that say so of him. Who are they?

MARIA They that add, moreover, he's drunk nightly in your company.

TOBY With drinking healths to my niece. I'll drink to her as long as there is a passage in my throat and drink in

37 Illyria. He's a coward and a coistrel that will not drink to

38 my niece till his brains turn o' th' toe like a parish top.

---

9 *finer* both 'tighter' and 'better'   11 *An* if   18 *tall* both 'tall' and 'brave'
23 *viol-de-gamboys* 'leg-viola,' predecessor of the violoncello   25 *without book* by memory   26 *natural* i.e. as a fool   28 *gust* taste   31 *substractors* detractors   37 *coistrel* horsegroom, base fellow   38 *parish* kept by the parish (?)

What, wench? Castiliano vulgo; for here comes Sir 39
Andrew Agueface.   40
    Enter Sir Andrew.

ANDREW Sir Toby Belch. How now, Sir Toby Belch?

TOBY Sweet Sir Andrew.

ANDREW Bless you, fair shrew.

MARIA And you too, sir.

TOBY Accost, Sir Andrew, accost.   45

ANDREW What's that?

TOBY My niece's chambermaid.

ANDREW Good Mistress Accost, I desire better acquaintance.

MARIA My name is Mary, sir.

ANDREW Good Mistress Mary Accost.

TOBY You mistake, knight. 'Accost' is front her, board 51
her, woo her, assail her.

ANDREW By my troth, I would not undertake her in this 53
company. Is that the meaning of 'accost'?

MARIA Fare you well, gentlemen.

TOBY An thou let part so, Sir Andrew, would thou
mightst never draw sword again.

ANDREW An you part so, mistress, I would I might never
draw sword again! Fair lady, do you think you have
fools in hand?

MARIA Sir, I have not you by th' hand.

ANDREW Marry, but you shall have, and here's my hand. 62

MARIA Now, sir, thought is free. I pray you, bring your
hand to th' butt'ry bar and let it drink.   64

ANDREW Wherefore, sweetheart? What's your meta·
phor?

MARIA It's dry, sir.   66

---

39 *Castiliano vulgo* (of doubtful meaning. Castilians were noted for decorum, and this may be a plea for 'common politeness.') **40** *Agueface* pale and thin-faced, like a man suffering from the acute fever of ague **45** *Accost* make up to (her) **51** *front* face; *board* greet (literally, go on board) **53** *undertake* (both literal and figurative senses intended) **62** *Marry* indeed, to be sure (originally an oath by the Virgin Mary) **64** *butt'ry* ale-cellar; *it* i.e. your hand **66** *dry* (a sign of age)

ANDREW Why, I think so. I am not such an ass but I can keep my hand dry. But what's your jest?

MARIA A dry jest, sir.

ANDREW Are you full of them?

MARIA Ay, sir, I have them at my fingers' ends. Marry,
72 now I let go your hand, I am barren.   *Exit.*

73 TOBY O knight, thou lack'st a cup of canary! When did I
74 see thee so put down?

ANDREW Never in your life, I think, unless you see canary put me down. Methinks sometimes I have no more wit than a Christian or an ordinary man has. But I am a great eater of beef, and I believe that does harm to my wit.

TOBY No question.

ANDREW An I thought that, I'd forswear it. I'll ride home to-morrow, Sir Toby.

82 TOBY Pourquoi, my dear knight?

ANDREW What is 'pourquoi'? Do, or not do? I would I
84 had bestowed that time in the tongues that I have in fencing, dancing, and bear-baiting. O, had I but fol-
86 lowed the arts!

TOBY Then hadst thou had an excellent head of hair.

88 ANDREW Why, would that have mended my hair?

TOBY Past question, for thou seest it will not curl by nature.

ANDREW But it becomes me well enough, does't not?

91 TOBY Excellent. It hangs like flax on a distaff; and I hope
92 to see a housewife take thee between her legs and spin it off.

ANDREW Faith, I'll home to-morrow, Sir Toby. Your niece will not be seen; or if she be, it's four to one she'll none of me. The Count himself here hard by woos her.

---

72 *barren* i.e. barren of jokes   73 *canary* a sweet wine from the Canary Islands   74 *put down* discomfited   82 *Pourquoi* why   84 *tongues* languages, perhaps with a pun on 'tongs,' curling irons   86 *arts* liberal arts such as languages   88 *mended* improved   91 *flax on a distaff* straight strings of flax on a stick used in spinning   92–93 *spin it off* lose hair as a result of venereal disease

TOBY She'll none o' th' Count. She'll not match above
her degree, neither in estate, years, nor wit; I have 98
heard her swear't. Tut, there's life in't, man.

ANDREW I'll stay a month longer. I am a fellow o' th'
strangest mind i' th' world. I delight in masques and
revels sometimes altogether.   102

TOBY Art thou good at these kickshawses, knight?   103

ANDREW As any man in Illyria, whatsoever he be, under
the degree of my betters, and yet I will not compare
with an old man.   106

TOBY What is thy excellence in a galliard, knight?   107

ANDREW Faith, I can cut a caper.   108

TOBY And I can cut the mutton to't.

ANDREW And I think I have the back-trick simply as   110
strong as any man in Illyria.

TOBY Wherefore are these things hid? Wherefore have
these gifts a curtain before 'em? Are they like to take 113
dust, like Mistress Mall's picture? Why dost thou not 114
go to church in a galliard and come home in a coranto? 115
My very walk should be a jig. I would not so much as
make water but in a sink-a-pace. What dost thou mean? 117
Is it a world to hide virtues in? I did think, by the excellent constitution of thy leg, it was formed under the star 119
of a galliard.

ANDREW Ay, 'tis strong, and it does indifferent well in a
dun-colored stock. Shall we set about some revels?   122

TOBY What shall we do else? Were we not born under
Taurus?   124

ANDREW Taurus? That's sides and heart.

---

98 *degree* position in society; *estate* fortune **102** *altogether* in all respects
103 *kickshawses* trifles (French '*quelque chose*') **106** *old man* probably 'ex-
perienced person' **107** *galliard* quick dance in triple time **108** *caper*
frolicsome leap; also a spice used with mutton **110** *back-trick* backward
step in a dance **113** *take* collect **114** *Mistress Mall's picture* any woman's
portrait **115** *coranto* swift running dance **117** *sink-a-pace* rapid dance of
five steps (French '*cinque-pas*') **119–20** *under . . . galliard* i.e. under a
dancing star **122** *stock* stocking **124** *Taurus* the Bull, one of the signs of
the Zodiac which governed the nose and throat

TOBY No, sir ; it is legs and thighs. Let me see thee caper.
Ha, higher ; ha, ha, excellent !　　　　　　　*Exeunt.*

*

I, iv　　　　*Enter Valentine, and Viola in man's attire.*

VALENTINE If the Duke continue these favors towards
you, Cesario, you are like to be much advanced. He hath
known you but three days and already you are no stranger.

4 VIOLA You either fear his humor or my negligence, that
you call in question the continuance of his love. Is he
inconstant, sir, in his favors ?

VALENTINE No, believe me.
　　　　Enter Duke, Curio, and Attendants.

VIOLA I thank you. Here comes the Count.

DUKE Who saw Cesario, ho ?

VIOLA On your attendance, my lord, here.

DUKE

11　Stand you awhile aloof. Cesario,

12　Thou know'st no less but all. I have unclasped
To thee the book even of my secret soul.

14　Therefore, good youth, address thy gait unto her ;
Be not denied access, stand at her doors,
And tell them there thy fixèd foot shall grow
Till thou have audience.

VIOLA　　　　　　　　　　Sure, my noble lord,
If she be so abandoned to her sorrow
As it is spoke, she never will admit me.

DUKE

Be clamorous and leap all civil bounds
Rather than make unprofited return.

VIOLA

Say I do speak with her, my lord, what then ?

I, iv The palace of Duke Orsino　4 *humor* changeableness　11 *you* i.e. all
except Cesario　12 *no less but all* everything　14 *address thy gait* direct your
steps

36

DUKE
O, then unfold the passion of my love;
Surprise her with discourse of my dear faith;
It shall become thee well to act my woes.
She will attend it better in thy youth
Than in a nuncio's of more grave aspect.   27

VIOLA
I think not so, my lord.

DUKE   Dear lad, believe it;
For they shall yet belie thy happy years
That say thou art a man. Diana's lip
Is not more smooth and rubious; thy small pipe   31
Is as the maiden's organ, shrill and sound,   32
And all is semblative a woman's part.   33
I know thy constellation is right apt   34
For this affair. Some four or five attend him,
All, if you will; for I myself am best
When least in company. Prosper well in this,
And thou shalt live as freely as thy lord
To call his fortunes thine.

VIOLA   I'll do my best
To woo your lady. *[aside]* Yet a barful strife!   40
Whoe'er I woo, myself would be his wife.   *Exeunt.*

*

Enter Maria and Clown.   I, v
MARIA Nay, either tell me where thou hast been, or I will
not open my lips so wide as a bristle may enter in way of
thy excuse. My lady will hang thee for thy absence.
CLOWN Let her hang me. He that is well hanged in this
world needs to fear no colors.   5

27 *nuncio's* messenger's   31 *rubious* ruby red; *pipe* throat, voice   32 *shrill
and sound* high and clear   33 *semblative* like   34 *constellation* predestined
nature   40 *barful strife* conflict full of hindrances
I, v Within the house of Olivia   5 *fear no colors* fear nothing (proverbial)

MARIA Make that good.

CLOWN He shall see none to fear.

8 MARIA A good lenten answer. I can tell thee where that saying was born, of 'I fear no colors.'

CLOWN Where, good Mistress Mary?

MARIA In the wars; and that may you be bold to say in your foolery.

CLOWN Well, God give them wisdom that have it, and those that are fools, let them use their talents.

MARIA Yet you will be hanged for being so long absent, or to be turned away. Is not that as good as a hanging to you?

CLOWN Many a good hanging prevents a bad marriage,
19 and for turning away, let summer bear it out.

MARIA You are resolute then?

21 CLOWN Not so, neither; but I am resolved on two points.

22 MARIA That if one break, the other will hold; or if both
23 break, your gaskins fall.

CLOWN Apt, in good faith; very apt. Well, go thy way! If Sir Toby would leave drinking, thou wert as witty a
26 piece of Eve's flesh as any in Illyria.

MARIA Peace, you rogue; no more o' that. Here comes my
28 lady. Make your excuse wisely, you were best.   [Exit.]
          Enter Lady Olivia with Malvolio.

CLOWN Wit, an't be thy will, put me into good fooling. Those wits that think they have thee do very oft prove fools, and I that am sure I lack thee may pass for a wise
32 man. For what says Quinapalus? 'Better a witty fool than a foolish wit.' God bless thee, lady.

OLIVIA Take the fool away.

CLOWN Do you not hear, fellows? Take away the lady.

---

8 *lenten* thin, scanty   19 *let . . . out* i.e. let mild weather make homelessness endurable   21 *points* laces fastening hose to doublet   22–23 *if one . . . fall* (Maria puns on *points*, see l. 21)   23 *gaskins* loose breeches   26 *Eve's flesh* erring woman   28 *you were best* it would be best for you   32 *Quinapalus* (an invention of the Clown)

OLIVIA Go to, y' are a dry fool! I'll no more of you. Be- 36
sides, you grow dishonest. 37
CLOWN Two faults, madonna, that drink and good coun- 38
sel will amend. For give the dry fool drink, then is the
fool not dry. Bid the dishonest man mend himself: if he 40
mend, he is no longer dishonest; if he cannot, let the
botcher mend him. Anything that's mended is but 42
patched; virtue that transgresses is but patched with
sin, and sin that amends is but patched with virtue. If
that this simple syllogism will serve, so; if it will not,
what remedy? As there is no true cuckold but calamity,
so beauty 's a flower. The lady bade take away the fool;
therefore, I say again, take her away.
OLIVIA Sir, I bade them take away you.
CLOWN Misprision in the highest degree. Lady, cucullus 50
non facit monachum. That's as much to say as, I wear
not motley in my brain. Good madonna, give me leave 52
to prove you a fool.
OLIVIA Can you do it?
CLOWN Dexteriously, good madonna. 55
OLIVIA Make your proof.
CLOWN I must catechize you for it, madonna. Good my
mouse of virtue, answer me. 58
OLIVIA Well, sir, for want of other idleness, I'll bide your
proof.
CLOWN Good madonna, why mourn'st thou?
OLIVIA Good fool, for my brother's death.
CLOWN I think his soul is in hell, madonna.
OLIVIA I know his soul is in heaven, fool.
CLOWN The more fool, madonna, to mourn for your
brother's soul, being in heaven. Take away the fool,
gentlemen.

---

36 *Go to* enough, cease; *dry* dull **37** *dishonest* unreliable **38** *madonna* my
lady **40** *dry* thirsty **42** *botcher* mender of clothes **50** *Misprision* error
50–51 *cucullus . . . monachum* the cowl doesn't make the monk **52** *motley*
clothing of a mixed color, worn by stage fools **55** *Dexteriously* (variant of
'dexterously') **58** *mouse* (term of endearment); *of virtue* virtuous

OLIVIA What think you of this fool, Malvolio? Doth he
not mend?

70 MALVOLIO Yes, and shall do till the pangs of death shake
him. Infirmity, that decays the wise, doth ever make the
better fool.

CLOWN God send you, sir, a speedy infirmity, for the
better increasing your folly. Sir Toby will be sworn that
I am no fox, but he will not pass his word for twopence
that you are no fool.

OLIVIA How say you to that, Malvolio?

MALVOLIO I marvel your ladyship takes delight in such a
barren rascal. I saw him put down the other day with an
ordinary fool that has no more brain than a stone. Look

81 you now, he's out of his guard already. Unless you laugh
82 and minister occasion to him, he is gagged. I protest I
take these wise men that crow so at these set kind of
84 fools no better than the fools' zanies.

OLIVIA O, you are sick of self-love, Malvolio, and taste
with a distempered appetite. To be generous, guiltless,
87 and of free disposition, is to take those things for birdbolts that you deem cannon bullets. There is no slander
89 in an allowed fool, though he do nothing but rail; nor no
railing in a known discreet man, though he do nothing
but reprove.

92 CLOWN Now Mercury indue thee with leasing, for thou
speak'st well of fools.

      Enter Maria.

MARIA Madam, there is at the gate a young gentleman
much desires to speak with you.

OLIVIA From the Count Orsino, is it?

MARIA I know not, madam. 'Tis a fair young man, and
well attended.

OLIVIA Who of my people hold him in delay?

---

81 *out of his guard* without a defense (of wit) 82 *minister occasion* give an
opportunity 84 *zanies* i.e. fools' assistants 87 *birdbolts* blunt-headed
arrows for shooting birds 89 *allowed* licensed 92 *Mercury* god of guile
and tricks; *indue . . . leasing* endow you with the art of casuistry

MARIA Sir Toby, madam, your kinsman.

OLIVIA Fetch him off, I pray you. He speaks nothing but madman. Fie on him! *[Exit Maria.]* Go you, Malvolio. If it be a suit from the Count, I am sick, or not at home. What you will, to dismiss it. *(Exit Malvolio.)* Now you see, sir, how your fooling grows old, and people dislike it. 105

CLOWN Thou hast spoke for us, madonna, as if thy eldest son should be a fool; whose skull Jove cram with brains, for – here he comes – one of thy kin has a most weak pia mater. 110

Enter Sir Toby.

OLIVIA By mine honor, half drunk. What is he at the gate, cousin?

TOBY A gentleman.

OLIVIA A gentleman? What gentleman?

TOBY 'Tis a gentleman here. A plague o' these pickle-herring! How now, sot?

CLOWN Good Sir Toby.

OLIVIA Cousin, cousin, how have you come so early by this lethargy?

TOBY Lechery? I defy lechery. There's one at the gate.

OLIVIA Ay, marry, what is he?

TOBY Let him be the devil an he will, I care not. Give me faith, say I. Well, it's all one. *Exit.* 123

OLIVIA What's a drunken man like, fool?

CLOWN Like a drowned man, a fool, and a madman. One draught above heat makes him a fool, the second mads him, and a third drowns him. 126

OLIVIA Go thou and seek the crowner, and let him sit o' my coz; for he's in the third degree of drink – he's drowned. Go look after him. 128

CLOWN He is but mad yet, madonna, and the fool shall look to the madman. *[Exit.]*

105 *old* stale   110 *pia mater* i.e. brain   123 *faith* i.e. to resist the devil
126 *above heat* above the amount to make him normally warm   128 *crowner* coroner   128–29 *sit o' my coz* hold an inquest on my kinsman (Sir Toby)

Enter Malvolio.

MALVOLIO Madam, yond young fellow swears he will
speak with you. I told him you were sick; he takes on
him to understand so much, and therefore comes to
speak with you. I told him you were asleep; he seems to
have a foreknowledge of that too, and therefore comes
to speak with you. What is to be said to him, lady? He's
fortified against any denial.

OLIVIA Tell him he shall not speak with me.

141 MALVOLIO Has been told so; and he says he'll stand at
142   your door like a sheriff's post, and be the supporter to a
bench, but he'll speak with you.

OLIVIA What kind o' man is he?

MALVOLIO Why, of mankind.

OLIVIA What manner of man?

MALVOLIO Of very ill manner. He'll speak with you,
will you or no.

OLIVIA Of what personage and years is he?

MALVOLIO Not yet old enough for a man nor young
151   enough for a boy; as a squash is before 'tis a peascod, or a
152   codling when 'tis almost an apple. 'Tis with him in
153   standing water, between boy and man. He is very well-
favored and he speaks very shrewishly. One would
think his mother's milk were scarce out of him.

OLIVIA Let him approach. Call in my gentlewoman.

MALVOLIO Gentlewoman, my lady calls.   *Exit.*

   Enter Maria.

OLIVIA Give me my veil; come, throw it o'er my face.
We'll once more hear Orsino's embassy.

   Enter Viola.

VIOLA The honorable lady of the house, which is she?

OLIVIA Speak to me; I shall answer for her. Your will?

---

141 *Has* he has (from 'h' has)   142 *sheriff's post* post before a sheriff's house
on which notices were posted   151 *squash* unripe pea pod; *peascod* ripe pea
pod   152 *codling* unripe apple   153 *standing water* the tide at ebb or flood
when it flows neither way

VIOLA Most radiant, exquisite, and unmatchable beauty
– I pray you tell me if this be the lady of the house, for I
never saw her. I would be loath to cast away my speech ;
for, besides that it is excellently well penned, I have
taken great pains to con it. Good beauties, let me sustain 166
no scorn. I am very comptible, even to the least sinister 167
usage.

OLIVIA Whence came you, sir ?

VIOLA I can say little more than I have studied, and that
question 's out of my part. Good gentle one, give me
modest assurance if you be the lady of the house, that I
may proceed in my speech.

OLIVIA Are you a comedian ?   174

VIOLA No, my profound heart ; and yet (by the very
fangs of malice I swear) I am not that I play. Are you
the lady of the house ?

OLIVIA If I do not usurp myself, I am.   178

VIOLA Most certain, if you are she, you do usurp yourself ; for what is yours to bestow is not yours to reserve.
But this is from my commission. I will on with my speech 181
in your praise and then show you the heart of my message.

OLIVIA Come to what is important in't. I forgive you the 183
praise.

VIOLA Alas, I took great pains to study it, and 'tis poetical.

OLIVIA It is the more like to be feigned ; I pray you keep
it in. I heard you were saucy at my gates ; and allowed
your approach rather to wonder at you than to hear you.
If you be not mad, be gone ; if you have reason, be 189
brief. 'Tis not that time of moon with me to make one in 190
so skipping a dialogue.   191

MARIA Will you hoist sail, sir ? Here lies your way.

VIOLA No, good swabber ; I am to hull here a little longer. 193

---

166 con memorize; sustain endure 167 comptible sensitive 174 comedian
actor 178 usurp supplant 181 from outside 183 forgive excuse 189
reason sanity 190 'Tis . . . me i.e. I am not in the mood 191 skipping
sprightly 193 swabber one who washes decks; hull float without sail

194   Some mollification for your giant, sweet lady. Tell me
       your mind. I am a messenger.

OLIVIA Sure you have some hideous matter to deliver,
197   when the courtesy of it is so fearful. Speak your office.

VIOLA It alone concerns your ear. I bring no overture of
199   war, no taxation of homage. I hold the olive in my hand.
       My words are as full of peace as matter.

OLIVIA Yet you began rudely. What are you? What
       would you?

VIOLA The rudeness that hath appeared in me have I
204   learned from my entertainment. What I am, and what I
205   would, are as secret as maidenhead: to your ears, divin-
       ity; to any other's, profanation.

OLIVIA Give us the place alone; we will hear this divinity.
       [Exit Maria.] Now, sir, what is your text?

VIOLA Most sweet lady –

OLIVIA A comfortable doctrine, and much may be said of
       it. Where lies your text?

VIOLA In Orsino's bosom.

OLIVIA In his bosom? In what chapter of his bosom?

214 VIOLA To answer by the method, in the first of his heart.

OLIVIA O, I have read it; it is heresy. Have you no more
       to say?

VIOLA Good madam, let me see your face.

OLIVIA Have you any commission from your lord to ne-
       gotiate with my face? You are now out of your text.
       But we will draw the curtain and show you the picture.
221   [Unveils.] Look you, sir, such a one I was this present.
       Is't not well done?

VIOLA Excellently done, if God did all.

224 OLIVIA 'Tis in grain, sir; 'twill endure wind and weather.

VIOLA
       'Tis beauty truly blent, whose red and white

---

194 *giant* i.e. the small Maria   197 *courtesy* formality; *office* business   199
taxation demand   204 *entertainment* reception   205 *divinity* a holy message
214 *To . . . method* to continue the figure   221 *this present* a minute ago
224 *in grain* fast dyed

Nature's own sweet and cunning hand laid on.   226
Lady, you are the cruell'st she alive
If you will lead these graces to the grave,
And leave the world no copy.

OLIVIA O, sir, I will not be so hard-hearted. I will give out
divers schedules of my beauty. It shall be inventoried,   231
and every particle and utensil labelled to my will: as,   232
item, two lips, indifferent red; item, two grey eyes, with   233
lids to them; item, one neck, one chin, and so forth.
Were you sent hither to praise me?

VIOLA
I see you what you are; you are too proud;
But if you were the devil, you are fair.   237
My lord and master loves you. O, such love
Could be but recompensed though you were crowned   239
The nonpareil of beauty.

OLIVIA   How does he love me?

VIOLA
With adorations, with fertile tears,   241
With groans that thunder love, with sighs of fire.

OLIVIA
Your lord does know my mind; I cannot love him.
Yet I suppose him virtuous, know him noble,
Of great estate, of fresh and stainless youth;
In voices well divulged, free, learned, and valiant,   246
And in dimension and the shape of nature
A gracious person. But yet I cannot love him.
He might have took his answer long ago.

VIOLA
If I did love you in my master's flame,
With such a suff'ring, such a deadly life,   251
In your denial I would find no sense;

226 *cunning* skillful 231 *schedules* lists 232 *utensil* article; *labelled to* added to 233 *item* namely; *indifferent* moderately 237 *if* even if 239 *but recompensed though* no more than repaid even though 241 *fertile* abundant 246 *In voices well divulged* in public opinion well reported 251 *deadly life* life which is like death

45

I would not understand it.

OLIVIA   Why, what would you?

VIOLA

254 Make me a willow cabin at your gate
And call upon my soul within the house;
256 Write loyal cantons of contemnèd love
And sing them loud even in the dead of night;
Hallo your name to the reverberate hills
259 And make the babbling gossip of the air
Cry out 'Olivia!' O, you should not rest
Between the elements of air and earth
But you should pity me.

OLIVIA
You might do much. What is your parentage?

VIOLA
Above my fortunes, yet my state is well.
I am a gentleman.

OLIVIA   Get you to your lord.
I cannot love him. Let him send no more,
Unless, perchance, you come to me again
To tell me how he takes it. Fare you well.
I thank you for your pains. Spend this for me.

VIOLA
270 I am no fee'd post, lady; keep your purse;
My master, not myself, lacks recompense.
Love make his heart of flint that you shall love;
And let your fervor, like my master's, be
Placed in contempt. Farewell, fair cruelty.   *Exit.*

OLIVIA
'What is your parentage?'
'Above my fortunes, yet my state is well.
I am a gentleman.' I'll be sworn thou art.
Thy tongue, thy face, thy limbs, actions, and spirit
279 Do give thee fivefold blazon. Not too fast; soft, soft,

---

254 *willow* symbol of grief for unrequited love   **256** *cantons* songs; *con-temnèd* rejected   **259** *babbling gossip* echo   **270** *fee'd post* messenger to be paid or tipped   **279** *blazon* shield or coat of arms in heraldry

Unless the master were the man. How now?   280
Even so quickly may one catch the plague?
Methinks I feel this youth's perfections
With an invisible and subtle stealth
To creep in at mine eyes. Well, let it be.
What ho, Malvolio!

Enter Malvolio.

MALVOLIO   Here, madam, at your service.

OLIVIA
Run after that same peevish messenger,
The County's man. He left this ring behind him,   287
Would I or not. Tell him I'll none of it.
Desire him not to flatter with his lord   289
Nor hold him up with hopes. I am not for him.
If that the youth will come this way to-morrow,
I'll give him reasons for't. Hie thee, Malvolio.

MALVOLIO
Madam, I will.   *Exit.*

OLIVIA
I do I know not what, and fear to find
Mine eye too great a flatterer for my mind.
Fate, show thy force; ourselves we do not owe.   296
What is decreed must be – and be this so!   *[Exit.]*

*

Enter Antonio and Sebastian.   II, i

ANTONIO Will you stay no longer? Nor will you not that
I go with you?

SEBASTIAN By your patience, no. My stars shine darkly 3
over me; the malignancy of my fate might perhaps dis-
temper yours. Therefore I shall crave of you your
leave, that I may bear my evils alone. It were a bad
recompense for your love to lay any of them on you.

280 *Unless . . . man* i.e. unless Orsino were Cesario   287 *County* count   289
flatter with encourage   296 *owe* own
II, i A lodging some distance from Orsino's court   3 *patience* leave

47

ANTONIO Let me yet know of you whither you are bound.

9 SEBASTIAN No, sooth, sir. My determinate voyage is
10 mere extravagancy. But I perceive in you so excellent a
    touch of modesty that you will not extort from me what I
12 am willing to keep in ; therefore it charges me in manners
    the rather to express myself. You must know of me then,
    Antonio, my name is Sebastian, which I called Roderigo.
15 My father was that Sebastian of Messaline whom I know
    you have heard of. He left behind him myself and a
17 sister, both born in an hour. If the heavens had been
    pleased, would we had so ended! But you, sir, altered
19 that, for some hour before you took me from the breach
    of the sea was my sister drowned.

ANTONIO Alas the day!

SEBASTIAN A lady, sir, though it was said she much re-
    sembled me, was yet of many accounted beautiful. But
24 though I could not with such estimable wonder overfar
25 believe that, yet thus far I will boldly publish her : she
    bore a mind that envy could not but call fair. She is
    drowned already, sir, with salt water, though I seem to
    drown her remembrance again with more.

29 ANTONIO Pardon me, sir, your bad entertainment.

30 SEBASTIAN O good Antonio, forgive me your trouble.

31 ANTONIO If you will not murder me for my love, let me
    be your servant.

SEBASTIAN If you will not undo what you have done,
34 that is, kill him whom you have recovered, desire it not.
    Fare ye well at once. My bosom is full of kindness, and I
36 am yet so near the manners of my mother that, upon the
    least occasion more, mine eyes will tell tales of me. I am
    bound to the Count Orsino's court. Farewell.   *Exit.*

---

9 *sooth* truly; *determinate* determined upon   10 *extravagancy* wandering
12 *it . . . manners* I am compelled in good manners   15 *Messaline* Messina
in Sicily   17 *in an hour* in the same hour   19–20 *the breach of the sea* the
breaking waves   24 *estimable wonder* admiring judgment   25 *publish* de-
scribe publicly   29 *entertainment* treatment as my guest   30 *your trouble*
for causing you trouble   31 *murder me for* be my death in return for   34
recovered saved   36–37 *so near . . . tales of me* so effeminate I shall weep

ANTONIO
The gentleness of all the gods go with thee.
I have many enemies in Orsino's court,
Else would I very shortly see thee there.
But come what may, I do adore thee so
That danger shall seem sport, and I will go.   *Exit.*

*

Enter Viola and Malvolio at several doors.   II, ii

MALVOLIO Were not you ev'n now with the Countess
Olivia?

VIOLA Even now, sir. On a moderate pace I have since
arrived but hither.

MALVOLIO She returns this ring to you, sir. You might
have saved me my pains, to have taken it away yourself.
She adds, moreover, that you should put your lord into
a desperate assurance she will none of him. And one   7
thing more, that you be never so hardy to come again in
his affairs, unless it be to report your lord's taking of
this. Receive it so.

VIOLA She took the ring of me. I'll none of it.

MALVOLIO Come, sir, you peevishly threw it to her, and
her will is, it should be so returned. If it be worth
stooping for, there it lies, in your eye; if not, be it his
that finds it.   *Exit.*

VIOLA
I left no ring with her. What means this lady?
Fortune forbid my outside have not charmed her.
She made good view of me; indeed, so much   18
That, as methought, her eyes had lost her tongue,   19
For she did speak in starts distractedly.
She loves me sure; the cunning of her passion   21
Invites me in this churlish messenger.

II, ii A street near Olivia's house   s.d. *several* different   7 *desperate*
without hope   18 *made good view of* looked intently at   19 *lost* caused her
to lose   21 *cunning* craftiness

None of my lord's ring? Why, he sent her none.
I am the man. If it be so, as 'tis,
Poor lady, she were better love a dream.
Disguise, I see thou art a wickedness
27   Wherein the pregnant enemy does much.
28   How easy is it for the proper false
29   In women's waxen hearts to set their forms!
Alas, our frailty is the cause, not we,
For such as we are made of, such we be.
32   How will this fadge? My master loves her dearly;
33   And I (poor monster) fond as much on him;
And she (mistaken) seems to dote on me.
What will become of this? As I am man,
36   My state is desperate for my master's love.
As I am woman (now alas the day!),
38   What thriftless sighs shall poor Olivia breathe?
O Time, thou must untangle this, not I;
It is too hard a knot for me t' untie.

                                        [Exit.]

*

II, iii   *Enter Sir Toby and Sir Andrew.*

TOBY Approach, Sir Andrew. Not to be abed after mid-
2   night is to be up betimes; and 'diluculo surgere,' thou
       know'st.
ANDREW Nay, by my troth, I know not, but I know to be
       up late is to be up late.
6 TOBY A false conclusion; I hate it as an unfilled can. To
       be up after midnight, and to go to bed then, is early; so
       that to go to bed after midnight is to go to bed betimes.

---

27 *pregnant enemy* resourceful Satan   28 *the proper false* deceivers who are
prepossessing in appearance   29 *forms* impressions (as of a seal)   32 *fadge*
turn out   33 *monster* (because both man and woman); *fond* dote   36
desperate hopeless   38 *thriftless* unprofitable
II, iii Within Olivia's house   2 *diluculo surgere [saluberrimum est]* to get
up at dawn is healthful (Lily's *Latin Grammar*)   6 *can* metal vessel for
holding liquor

Does not our lives consist of the four elements?

ANDREW Faith, so they say; but I think it rather consists of eating and drinking.

TOBY Th' art a scholar! Let us therefore eat and drink. Marian I say! a stoup of wine!   13

Enter Clown.

ANDREW Here comes the fool, i' faith.

CLOWN How now, my hearts? Did you never see the pic-   15
ture of We Three?

TOBY Welcome, ass. Now let's have a catch.   17

ANDREW By my troth, the fool has an excellent breast. I   18
had rather than forty shillings I had such a leg, and so
sweet a breath to sing, as the fool has. In sooth, thou
wast in very gracious fooling last night, when thou   21
spok'st of Pigrogromitus, of the Vapians passing the   22
equinoctial of Queubus. 'Twas very good, i' faith. I
sent thee sixpence for thy leman. Hadst it?   24

CLOWN I did impeticos thy gratillity, for Malvolio's nose   25
is no whipstock. My lady has a white hand, and the Myr-   26
midons are no bottle-ale houses.

ANDREW Excellent. Why, this is the best fooling, when
all is done. Now a song!

TOBY Come on! there is sixpence for you. Let's have a
song.

ANDREW There's a testril of me too. If one knight give a–   31

CLOWN Would you have a love song, or a song of good   32
life?

TOBY A love song, a love song.

ANDREW Ay, ay, I care not for good life.

---

13 *stoup* goblet   15 *hearts* (term of endearment)   15–16 *picture of We Three* picture showing two fools or asses inscribed 'We Three,' the onlooker making the third   17 *catch* round-song (such as 'Three Blind Mice')   18 *breast* voice   21 *gracious* elegant   22–23 *Pigrogromitus . . . Queubus* (meaningless mock-learning)   24 *leman* sweetheart   25 *impeticos* put in pocket of gown; *gratillity* gratuity   26 *Myrmidons* Thessalian warriors (meaningless here)   31 *testril* tester, sixpence   32–33 *good life* virtuous living

Clown sings.

O mistress mine, where are you roaming ?
O, stay and hear ! your true-love's coming,
    That can sing both high and low.
Trip no further, pretty sweeting ;
40   Journeys end in lovers meeting,
    Every wise man's son doth know.

ANDREW Excellent good, i' faith.
TOBY Good, good.

Clown [sings].

What is love ? 'Tis not hereafter ;
Present mirth hath present laughter ;
    What's to come is still unsure :
In delay there lies no plenty ;
Then come kiss me, sweet and twenty,
    Youth's a stuff will not endure.

ANDREW A mellifluous voice, as I am true knight.
TOBY A contagious breath.
ANDREW Very sweet and contagious, i' faith.
TOBY To hear by the nose, it is dulcet in contagion. But
54 shall we make the welkin dance indeed ? Shall we rouse
the night owl in a catch that will draw three souls out of
56 one weaver ? Shall we do that ?
ANDREW An you love me, let's do't. I am dog at a catch.
CLOWN By'r Lady, sir, and some dogs will catch well.
ANDREW Most certain. Let our catch be 'Thou knave.'
CLOWN 'Hold thy peace, thou knave,' knight ? I shall be
constrained in't to call thee knave, knight.
ANDREW 'Tis not the first time I have constrained one to
call me knave. Begin, fool. It begins, 'Hold thy peace.'
CLOWN I shall never begin if I hold my peace.

54 *welkin* sky   56 *weaver* (weavers were famous for psalm-singing)

ANDREW Good, i' faith! Come, begin.
　　Catch sung. Enter Maria.
MARIA What a caterwauling do you keep here? If my
　　lady have not called up her steward Malvolio and bid
　　him turn you out of doors, never trust me.
TOBY My lady's a Cataian, we are politicians, Malvolio's 69
　　a Peg-a-Ramsey, and [sings] 'Three merry men be we.' 70
　　Am not I consanguineous? Am I not of her blood? 71
　　Tilly-vally, lady. [sings] 'There dwelt a man in Babylon, 72
　　lady, lady.'
CLOWN Beshrew me, the knight's in admirable fooling.
ANDREW Ay, he does well enough if he be disposed, and
　　so do I too. He does it with a better grace, but I do it
　　more natural.　　　　　　　　　　　　　　　　　77
TOBY [sings]
　　'O the twelfth day of December.'
MARIA For the love o' God, peace!
　　Enter Malvolio.
MALVOLIO My masters, are you mad? Or what are you?
　　Have you no wit, manners, nor honesty, but to gabble
　　like tinkers at this time of night? Do ye make an alehouse
　　of my lady's house, that ye squeak out your coziers' 83
　　catches without any mitigation or remorse of voice? Is 84
　　there no respect of place, persons, nor time in you?
TOBY We did keep time, sir, in our catches. Sneck up. 86
MALVOLIO Sir Toby, I must be round with you. My lady 87
　　bade me tell you that, though she harbors you as her
　　kinsman, she's nothing allied to your disorders. If you
　　can separate yourself and your misdemeanors, you are
　　welcome to the house. If not, and it would please you to
　　take leave of her, she is very willing to bid you farewell.

---

69 *Cataian* native of Cathay, trickster; *politicians* intriguers **70** *Peg-a-Ramsey* characters in an old song, here used as a term of contempt **71** *consanguineous* related **72** *Tilly-vally* nonsense **72–73** *There dwelt . . .* (from an old song, 'The Constancy of Susanna') **77** *natural* naturally (but the word also means 'like a fool') **83** *coziers'* cobblers' **84** *mitigation or remorse* i.e. considerate lowering **86** *Sneck up* go hang **87** *round* plain

TOBY [*sings*]
93   'Farewell, dear heart since I must needs be gone.'
MARIA Nay, good Sir Toby.
CLOWN [*sings*]
   'His eyes do show his days are almost done.'
MALVOLIO Is't even so?
TOBY [*sings*]
   'But I will never die.'
CLOWN [*sings*]
   Sir Toby, there you lie.
MALVOLIO This is much credit to you.
TOBY [*sings*]
   'Shall I bid him go?'
CLOWN [*sings*]
   'What an if you do?'
TOBY [*sings*]
   'Shall I bid him go, and spare not?'
CLOWN [*sings*]
   'O, no, no, no, no, you dare not!'
TOBY Out o' tune, sir? Ye lie. Art any more than a steward? Dost thou think, because thou art virtuous, there shall be no more cakes and ale?
107 CLOWN Yes, by Saint Anne, and ginger shall be hot i' th' mouth too.
109 TOBY Th' art i' th' right. – Go, sir, rub your chain with crumbs. A stoup of wine, Maria!
MALVOLIO Mistress Mary, if you prized my lady's favor
112   at anything more than contempt, you would not give means for this uncivil rule. She shall know of it, by this hand.   *Exit.*
115 MARIA Go shake your ears.
ANDREW 'Twere as good a deed as to drink when a man's

---

93 *Farewell, dear heart* . . . (from an old song, 'Corydon's Farewell to Phyllis') 107 *ginger* (used to spice ale) 109–10 *rub . . . crumbs* (a contemptuous allusion to his steward's chain) 112–13 *give means* i.e. bring the wine 115 *your ears* i.e. your ass's ears

ahungry, to challenge him the field, and then to break
promise with him and make a fool of him.

TOBY Do't, knight. I'll write thee a challenge; or I'll deliver thy indignation to him by word of mouth.

MARIA Sweet Sir Toby, be patient for to-night. Since the
youth of the Count's was to-day with my lady, she is
much out of quiet. For Monsieur Malvolio, let me alone
with him. If I do not gull him into a nayword, and make 124
him a common recreation, do not think I have wit 125
enough to lie straight in my bed. I know I can do it.

TOBY Possess us, possess us. Tell us something of him. 127

MARIA Marry, sir, sometimes he is a kind of Puritan.

ANDREW O, if I thought that, I'd beat him like a dog.

TOBY What, for being a Puritan? Thy exquisite reason,
dear knight.

ANDREW I have no exquisite reason for't, but I have
reason good enough.

MARIA The devil a Puritan that he is, or anything con-
stantly but a time-pleaser; an affectioned ass, that cons 135
state without book and utters it by great swarths; the 136
best persuaded of himself; so crammed, as he thinks,
with excellencies that it is his grounds of faith that all
that look on him love him; and on that vice in him will
my revenge find notable cause to work.

TOBY What wilt thou do?

MARIA I will drop in his way some obscure epistles of
love, wherein by the color of his beard, the shape of his
leg, the manner of his gait, the expressure of his eye, 144
forehead, and complexion, he shall find himself most
feelingly personated. I can write very like my lady your 146
niece; on a forgotten matter we can hardly make distinction of our hands.

---

124 *gull* trick; *nayword* byword   125 *recreation* amusement   127 *Possess us*
give us the facts   135 *time-pleaser* sycophant; *affectioned* affected   135–36
cons . . . book learns a stately manner by heart   136 *swarths* quantities
144 *expressure* expression   146 *personated* represented

TOBY Excellent. I smell a device.

ANDREW I have't in my nose too.

TOBY He shall think by the letters that thou wilt drop
that they come from my niece, and that she's in love
with him.

MARIA My purpose is indeed a horse of that color.

ANDREW And your horse now would make him an ass.

MARIA Ass, I doubt not.

ANDREW O, 'twill be admirable.

MARIA Sport royal, I warrant you. I know my physic will
work with him. I will plant you two, and let the fool
make a third, where he shall find the letter. Observe his

161   construction of it. For this night, to bed, and dream on
162   the event. Farewell.   *Exit.*

163 TOBY Good night, Penthesilea.

164 ANDREW Before me, she's a good wench.

165 TOBY She's a beagle true-bred, and one that adores me.
What o' that?

ANDREW I was adored once too.

TOBY Let's to bed, knight. Thou hadst need send for
more money.

170 ANDREW If I cannot recover your niece, I am a foul way
171   out.

TOBY Send for money, knight. If thou hast her not i' th'
173   end, call me Cut.

ANDREW If I do not, never trust me, take it how you will.

175 TOBY Come, come; I'll go burn some sack. 'Tis too late
to go to bed now. Come, knight; come, knight. *Exeunt.*

*

161 *construction* interpretation   **162** *event* outcome   **163** *Penthesilea* queen
of the Amazons   **164** *Before me* I swear by myself   **165** *beagle* small
rabbit-hound   **170** *recover* gain   **171** *out* out of money   **173** *Cut* horse
with a docked tail   **175** *burn some sack* warm some sherry

Enter Duke, Viola, Curio, and others. II, iv

DUKE

    Give me some music. Now good morrow, friends.

    Now, good Cesario, but that piece of song,

    That old and antique song we heard last night.   3

    Methought it did relieve my passion much,

    More than light airs and recollected terms   5

    Of these most brisk and giddy-pacèd times.

    Come, but one verse.

CURIO He is not here, so please your lordship, that should
    sing it.

DUKE Who was it?

CURIO Feste the jester, my lord, a fool that the Lady
    Olivia's father took much delight in. He is about the
    house.

DUKE

    Seek him out, and play the tune the while.

[Exit Curio.]

    Music plays.

    Come hither, boy. If ever thou shalt love,

    In the sweet pangs of it remember me;

    For such as I am all true lovers are,

    Unstaid and skittish in all motions else   17

    Save in the constant image of the creature

    That is beloved. How dost thou like this tune?

VIOLA

    It gives a very echo to the seat   20

    Where Love is throned.

DUKE   Thou dost speak masterly.

    My life upon't, young though thou art, thine eye

    Hath stayed upon some favor that it loves.   23

    Hath it not, boy?

VIOLA   A little, by your favor.

II, iv Within the palace of Orsino   **3** *antique* quaint   **5** *recollected* studied
17 *motions* emotions   **20–21** *the seat … throned* i.e. the heart   **23** *favor* face

DUKE
What kind of woman is't?

VIOLA   Of your complexion.

DUKE
She is not worth thee then. What years, i' faith?

VIOLA
About your years, my lord.

DUKE
Too old, by heaven. Let still the woman take
29 An elder than herself: so wears she to him,
30 So sways she level in her husband's heart;
For, boy, however we do praise ourselves,
32 Our fancies are more giddy and unfirm,
More longing, wavering, sooner lost and worn,
Than women's are.

VIOLA   I think it well, my lord.

DUKE
Then let thy love be younger than thyself,
36 Or thy affection cannot hold the bent;
For women are as roses, whose fair flow'r,
Being once displayed, doth fall that very hour.

VIOLA
And so they are; alas, that they are so.
To die, even when they to perfection grow.
          Enter Curio and Clown.

DUKE
O, fellow, come, the song we had last night.
Mark it, Cesario; it is old and plain.
43 The spinsters and the knitters in the sun,
44 And the free maids that weave their thread with bones,
45 Do use to chant it. It is silly sooth,
And dallies with the innocence of love,
47 Like the old age.

---

29 *wears* adapts herself   30 *sways . . . heart* she keeps constant her husband's
love   32 *fancies* loves   36 *bent* direction   43 *spinsters* spinners   44 *free*
innocent; *bones* bone bobbins   45 *Do use* are accustomed; *silly sooth* simple
truth   47 *old age* good old days

CLOWN Are you ready, sir?
DUKE I prithee sing.
          Music.

                      The Song.

Come away, come away, death,
     And in sad cypress let me be laid.   51
Fly away, fly away, breath;
     I am slain by a fair cruel maid.
My shroud of white, stuck all with yew,   54
     O, prepare it.
My part of death, no one so true   56
     Did share it.

Not a flower, not a flower sweet,
     On my black coffin let there be strown;
Not a friend, not a friend greet
     My poor corpse, where my bones shall be thrown.
A thousand thousand sighs to save,
     Lay me, O, where
Sad true lover never find my grave,
     To weep there.

DUKE There's for thy pains.
CLOWN No pains, sir. I take pleasure in singing, sir.
DUKE I'll pay thy pleasure then.
CLOWN Truly, sir, and pleasure will be paid one time or   69
     another.
DUKE Give me now leave to leave thee.
CLOWN Now the melancholy god protect thee, and the
     tailor make thy doublet of changeable taffeta, for thy   73
     mind is a very opal. I would have men of such constancy
     put to sea, that their business might be everything, and
     their intent everywhere; for that's it that always makes a
     good voyage of nothing. Farewell.   *Exit.*   77

51 *cypress* coffin of cypress wood   54 *yew* yew sprigs, associated with
mourning   56 *part* portion   69 *pleasure…paid* indulgence exacts its penalty
73 *changeable* i.e. opalescent in effect   77 *nothing* bringing back nothing

DUKE

78   Let all the rest give place.

                              [*Exeunt Curio and Attendants.*]
                              Once more, Cesario,

79   Get thee to yond same sovereign cruelty.
      Tell her, my love, more noble than the world,
      Prizes not quantity of dirty lands ;

82   The parts that fortune hath bestowed upon her
      Tell her I hold as giddily as fortune,
      But 'tis that miracle and queen of gems

85   That nature pranks her in attracts my soul.

VIOLA

      But if she cannot love you, sir ?

DUKE

      I cannot be so answered.

VIOLA   Sooth, but you must.
      Say that some lady, as perhaps there is,
      Hath for your love as great a pang of heart
      As you have for Olivia. You cannot love her.
      You tell her so. Must she not then be answered ?

DUKE

      There is no woman's sides

93   Can bide the beating of so strong a passion
      As love doth give my heart ; no woman's heart

95   So big to hold so much ; they lack retention.
      Alas, their love may be called appetite,

97   No motion of the liver but the palate,

98   That suffers surfeit, cloyment, and revolt ;
      But mine is all as hungry as the sea
      And can digest as much. Make no compare
      Between that love a woman can bear me

102   And that I owe Olivia.

VIOLA   Ay, but I know.

---

78 *give place* leave   **79** *sovereign cruelty* supremely cruel person   **82** *parts*
possessions   **85** *pranks* decks   **93** *bide* withstand   **95** *retention* capacity
of retaining   **97** *motion* emotion; *liver* seat of the emotion of love   **98**
revolt revulsion   **102** *owe* have toward

DUKE
  What dost thou know?
VIOLA
  Too well what love women to men may owe.
  In faith, they are as true of heart as we.
  My father had a daughter loved a man
  As it might be perhaps, were I a woman,
  I should your lordship.
DUKE   And what's her history?
VIOLA
  A blank, my lord. She never told her love,
  But let concealment, like a worm i' th' bud,
  Feed on her damask cheek. She pined in thought;   111
  And, with a green and yellow melancholy,
  She sat like Patience on a monument,
  Smiling at grief. Was not this love indeed?
  We men may say more, swear more; but indeed
  Our shows are more than will; for still we prove   116
  Much in our vows but little in our love.
DUKE
  But died thy sister of her love, my boy?
VIOLA
  I am all the daughters of my father's house,
  And all the brothers too, and yet I know not.
  Sir, shall I to this lady?
DUKE   Ay, that's the theme.
  To her in haste. Give her this jewel. Say
  My love can give no place, bide no denay.   *Exeunt.* 123

                    *

      Enter Sir Toby, Sir Andrew, and Fabian.   II, v
TOBY Come thy ways, Signior Fabian.
FABIAN Nay, I'll come. If I lose a scruple of this sport, let 2
  me be boiled to death with melancholy.

111 *damask* pink and white, as of a damask rose   116 *will* our passions
123 *can give no place* cannot yield; *denay* denial
II, v The garden of Olivia's house   2 *scruple* bit

TOBY Wouldst thou not be glad to have the niggardly
5   rascally sheep-biter come by some notable shame?
FABIAN I would exult, man. You know he brought me
     out o' favor with my lady about a bear-baiting here.
TOBY To anger him we'll have the bear again, and we will
     fool him black and blue. Shall we not, Sir Andrew?
ANDREW An we do not, it is pity of our lives.
       Enter Maria.
11   TOBY Here comes the little villain. How now, my metal
     of India?
13   MARIA Get ye all three into the box tree. Malvolio 's
     coming down this walk. He has been yonder i' the sun
15   practicing behavior to his own shadow this half hour.
     Observe him, for the love of mockery; for I know this
17   letter will make a contemplative idiot of him. Close, in
     the name of jesting. *[The others hide.]* Lie thou there
     [throws down a letter] ; for here comes the trout that
20   must be caught with tickling.   *Exit.*
       Enter Malvolio.
MALVOLIO 'Tis but fortune; all is fortune. Maria once
22   told me she did affect me; and I have heard herself come
     thus near, that, should she fancy, it should be one of my
24   complexion. Besides, she uses me with a more exalted
25   respect than any one else that follows her. What should
     I think on't?
TOBY Here's an overweening rogue.
FABIAN O, peace! Contemplation makes a rare turkey
29   cock of him. How he jets under his advanced plumes!
30   ANDREW 'Slight, I could so beat the rogue.
TOBY Peace, I say.
MALVOLIO To be Count Malvolio.
TOBY Ah, rogue!

---

5 *sheep-biter* dog that bites sheep, sneaking fellow   11–12 *my metal of India*
my golden one   13 *tree* i.e. hedge   15 *behavior* elegant conduct   17
contemplative idiot i.e. addled by his musings; *Close* hide   20 *tickling*
stroking about the gills   22 *she did affect me* Olivia liked me   24 *complexion*
personality   25 *that follows her* in her service   29 *jets* struts   30 *'Slight*
an oath (by God's light)

ANDREW Pistol him, pistol him.

TOBY Peace, peace.

MALVOLIO There is example for't. The Lady of the 36
Strachy married the yeoman of the wardrobe.

ANDREW Fie on him, Jezebel. 38

FABIAN O, peace! Now he's deeply in. Look how imagination blows him. 40

MALVOLIO Having been three months married to her,
sitting in my state – 42

TOBY O for a stone-bow, to hit him in the eye! 43

MALVOLIO Calling my officers about me, in my branched 44
velvet gown; having come from a day-bed, where I 45
have left Olivia sleeping –

TOBY Fire and brimstone!

FABIAN O, peace, peace!

MALVOLIO And then to have the humor of state; and 49
after a demure travel of regard, telling them I know my 50
place, as I would they should do theirs, to ask for my
kinsman Toby –

TOBY Bolts and shackles!

FABIAN O peace, peace, peace, now, now.

MALVOLIO Seven of my people, with an obedient start,
make out for him. I frown the while, and perchance
wind up my watch, or play with my – some rich jewel.
Toby approaches; curtsies there to me –

TOBY Shall this fellow live?

FABIAN Though our silence be drawn from us with cars, 60
yet peace.

MALVOLIO I extend my hand to him thus, quenching my
familiar smile with an austere regard of control – 63

TOBY And does not Toby take you a blow o' the lips then? 64

MALVOLIO Saying, 'Cousin Toby, my fortunes having

36–37 *Lady of the Strachy* (unidentified allusion)   38 *Jezebel* wicked queen
of Israel   40 *blows him* puffs him up   42 *state* chair of state   43 *stone-bow*
stone-shooter   44 *branched* embroidered   45 *day-bed* sofa   49 *humor of
state* manner and disposition of authority   50 *demure . . . regard* grave
survey   60 *with cars* by force   63 *regard of control* look of authority
64 *take* give

cast me on your niece, give me this prerogative of
speech.'

TOBY What, what?

MALVOLIO 'You must amend your drunkenness.'

TOBY Out, scab!

FABIAN Nay, patience, or we break the sinews of our plot.

MALVOLIO 'Besides, you waste the treasure of your time
with a foolish knight' –

ANDREW That's me, I warrant you.

MALVOLIO 'One Sir Andrew' –

ANDREW I knew 'twas I, for many do call me fool.

MALVOLIO What employment have we here?
                    [Takes up the letter.]

77 FABIAN Now is the woodcock near the gin.

TOBY O, peace, and the spirit of humors intimate reading
aloud to him!

MALVOLIO By my life, this is my lady's hand. These be
her very C's, her U's, and her T's; and thus makes she
82 her great P's. It is, in contempt of question, her hand.

ANDREW Her C's, her U's, and her T's? Why that?

MALVOLIO *[reads]* 'To the unknown beloved, this, and
85 my good wishes.' Her very phrases! By your leave, wax.

86 Soft, and the impressure her Lucrece, with which she
uses to seal. 'Tis my lady. To whom should this be?

88 FABIAN This wins him, liver and all.

MALVOLIO *[reads]*
           'Jove knows I love,
                    But who?
           Lips, do not move;
                    No man must know.'

93   'No man must know.' What follows? The numbers
altered! 'No man must know.' If this should be thee,
Malvolio?

---

77 *woodcock* (a stupid bird); *gin* snare, trap   82 *in contempt of* beyond
85 *By . . . wax* (a conventional apology for breaking a seal)   86 *Soft* careful,
slow; *Lucrece* (her seal was a likeness of the chaste Lucrece)   88 *liver* the
seat of passion   93 *numbers* metre

TOBY Marry, hang thee, brock!   96
MALVOLIO *[reads]*
          'I may command where I adore,
              But silence, like a Lucrece knife,
              With bloodless stroke my heart doth gore.
              M. O. A. I. doth sway my life.'
FABIAN A fustian riddle.   101
TOBY Excellent wench, say I.   102
MALVOLIO 'M. O. A. I. doth sway my life.' Nay, but
    first, let me see, let me see, let me see.
FABIAN What dish o' poison has she dressed him!   105
TOBY And with what wing the staniel checks at it!   106
MALVOLIO 'I may command where I adore.' Why, she
    may command me: I serve her; she is my lady. Why,
    this is evident to any formal capacity. There is no ob-   109
    struction in this. And the end; what should that alpha-
    betical position portend? If I could make that resemble
    something in me! Softly, 'M. O. A. I.'
TOBY O, ay, make up that. He is now at a cold scent.   113
FABIAN Sowter will cry upon't for all this, though it be as   114
    rank as a fox.
MALVOLIO M. – Malvolio. M. – Why, that begins my
    name.
FABIAN Did not I say he would work it out? The cur is
    excellent at faults.   118
MALVOLIO M. – But then there is no consonancy in the   119
    sequel. That suffers under probation. A should follow,   120
    but O does.
FABIAN And O shall end, I hope.
TOBY Ay, or I'll cudgel him, and make him cry O.
MALVOLIO And then I comes behind.
FABIAN Ay, an you had any eye behind you, you might see

96 *brock* badger 101 *fustian* ridiculously lofty 102 *Excellent wench* clever
girl (Maria) 105 *dressed* prepared 106 *staniel* an inferior hawk; *checks*
turns to pursue the wrong prey 109 *formal* normal; *obstruction* difficulty
113 *cold scent* difficult trail 114 *Sowter . . . upon't* the hound will pick up
the scent 118 *faults* gaps or breaks in the scent 119 *consonancy* agreement
120 *suffers* becomes strained; *probation* testing

more detraction at your heels than fortunes before you.

127 MALVOLIO M, O, A, I. This simulation is not as the for-
128 mer; and yet, to crush this a little, it would bow to me,
for every one of these letters are in my name. Soft, here
follows prose.

131 *[Reads]* 'If this fall into thy hand, revolve. In my stars I
am above thee, but be not afraid of greatness. Some are
born great, some achieve greatness, and some have greatness thrust upon 'em. Thy Fates open their hands; let
135 thy blood and spirit embrace them; and to inure thyself
136 to what thou art like to be, cast thy humble slough and
appear fresh. Be opposite with a kinsman, surly with
138 servants. Let thy tongue tang arguments of state; put
139 thyself into the trick of singularity. She thus advises thee
that sighs for thee. Remember who commended thy yel-
141 low stockings and wished to see thee ever cross-gartered.
I say, remember. Go to, thou art made, if thou desir'st
to be so. If not, let me see thee a steward still, the fellow
of servants, and not worthy to touch Fortune's fingers.
Farewell. She that would alter services with thee,
146   'The Fortunate Unhappy.'
147 Daylight and champian discovers not more. This is open.
148 I will be proud, I will read politic authors, I will baffle Sir
149 Toby, I will wash off gross acquaintance, I will be point-
devise, the very man. I do not now fool myself, to let
151 imagination jade me, for every reason excites to this, that
my lady loves me. She did commend my yellow stockings of late, she did praise my leg being cross-gartered;
and in this she manifests herself to my love, and with a
155 kind of injunction drives me to these habits of her liking.

---

127 *simulation* hidden meaning   **128** *crush* force   **131** *revolve* consider;
stars fate   **135** *inure* accustom   **136** *slough* outer skin   **138** *tang* sound with
139 *singularity* eccentricity   **141** *cross-gartered* wearing hose-garters
crossed above and below the knee   **146** *Unhappy* unfortunate   **147**
champian open country; *discovers* reveals, discloses   **148** *politic authors*
writers on government; *baffle* subject to disgrace   **149–50** *point-devise*
perfectly correct   **151** *jade* trick   **155** *habits* attire

I thank my stars, I am happy. I will be strange, stout, in 156
yellow stockings, and cross-gartered, even with the
swiftness of putting on. Jove and my stars be praised.
Here is yet a postscript.
[Reads] 'Thou canst not choose but know who I am. If
thou entertain'st my love, let it appear in thy smiling. 161
Thy smiles become thee well. Therefore in my presence
still smile, dear my sweet, I prithee.'
Jove, I thank thee. I will smile; I will do everything that
thou wilt have me.   *Exit.*

FABIAN I will not give my part of this sport for a pension
of thousands to be paid from the Sophy.   167

TOBY I could marry this wench for this device.

ANDREW So could I too.

TOBY And ask no other dowry with her but such another jest.
Enter Maria.

ANDREW Nor I neither.

FABIAN Here comes my noble gull-catcher.   173

TOBY Wilt thou set thy foot o' my neck?

ANDREW Or o' mine either?

TOBY Shall I play my freedom at tray-trip and become 176
thy bondslave?

ANDREW I' faith, or I either?

TOBY Why, thou hast put him in such a dream that,
when the image of it leaves him, he must run mad.

MARIA Nay, but say true, does it work upon him?

TOBY Like aqua-vitae with a midwife.   182

MARIA If you will, then, see the fruits of the sport, mark
his first approach before my lady. He will come to her in
yellow stockings, and 'tis a color she abhors, and cross-
gartered, a fashion she detests; and he will smile upon
her, which will now be so unsuitable to her disposition,
being addicted to a melancholy as she is, that it cannot

---

156 *strange* aloof; *stout* proud **161** *entertain'st* accept **167** *Sophy* shah of
Persia **173** *gull-catcher* fool-catcher **176** *play* gamble; *tray-trip* a game
of dice **182** *aqua-vitae* any distilled liquor

but turn him into a notable contempt. If you will see it,
follow me.

190 TOBY To the gates of Tartar, thou most excellent devil of
wit.

ANDREW I'll make one too.   *Exeunt.*

*

III, i   *Enter Viola and Clown [with a tabor].*

1 VIOLA Save thee, friend, and thy music. Dost thou live by
2   thy tabor?

CLOWN No, sir, I live by the church.

VIOLA Art thou a churchman?

CLOWN No such matter, sir. I do live by the church; for I
do live at my house, and my house doth stand by the
church.

8 VIOLA So thou mayst say, the king lies by a beggar, if a
beggar dwell near him; or, the church stands by thy
tabor, if thy tabor stand by the church.

CLOWN You have said, sir. To see this age! A sentence is
12   but a chev'ril glove to a good wit. How quickly the
wrong side may be turned outward!

14 VIOLA Nay, that's certain. They that dally nicely with
15   words may quickly make them wanton.

CLOWN I would therefore my sister had had no name, sir.

VIOLA Why, man?

CLOWN Why, sir, her name's a word, and to dally with
19   that word might make my sister wanton. But indeed
20   words are very rascals since bonds disgraced them.

VIOLA Thy reason, man?

CLOWN Troth, sir, I can yield you none without words,
and words are grown so false I am loath to prove reason
with them.

190 *Tartar* Tartarus, the section of hell reserved for the most evil
III, i Before the house of Olivia 1 *Save thee* God save thee; *live by* make
a living with 2 *tabor* drum 8 *lies* dwells 12 *chev'ril* kid 14 *dally
nicely* play subtly 15 *wanton* capricious 19 *wanton* abandoned 20 *since
... them* i.e. since bonds have been needed to guarantee them

VIOLA I warrant thou art a merry fellow and car'st for
   nothing.

CLOWN Not so, sir; I do care for something; but in my
   conscience, sir, I do not care for you. If that be to care
   for nothing, sir, I would it would make you invisible.

VIOLA Art not thou the Lady Olivia's fool?

CLOWN No, indeed, sir. The Lady Olivia has no folly.
   She will keep no fool, sir, till she be married; and fools
   are as like husbands as pilchers are to herrings, the 33
   husband's the bigger. I am indeed not her fool, but her
   corrupter of words.

VIOLA I saw thee late at the Count Orsino's.

CLOWN Foolery, sir, does walk about the orb like the sun;
   it shines everywhere. I would be sorry, sir, but the fool
   should be as oft with your master as with my mistress. I
   think I saw your wisdom there.

VIOLA Nay, an thou pass upon me, I'll no more with thee. 41
   Hold, there's expenses for thee.
         [Gives a coin.]

CLOWN Now Jove, in his next commodity of hair, send 43
   thee a beard.

VIOLA By my troth, I'll tell thee, I am almost sick for one,
   though I would not have it grow on my chin. Is thy lady
   within?

CLOWN Would not a pair of these have bred, sir?

VIOLA Yes, being kept together and put to use. 49

CLOWN I would play Lord Pandarus of Phrygia, sir, to 50
   bring a Cressida to this Troilus.

VIOLA I understand you, sir. 'Tis well begged.
         [Gives another coin.]

CLOWN The matter, I hope, is not great, sir, begging but
   a beggar: Cressida was a beggar. My lady is within, sir. 54

---

33 *pilchers* pilchards (small fish resembling herring) 41 *pass upon* jest at
43 *commodity* shipment 49 *put to use* put out at interest 50 *Pandarus* the
go-between in the tale told by Chaucer and others 54 *Cressida was a
beggar* (she became a leprous beggar in Henryson's continuation of
Chaucer's story)

55 I will conster to them whence you come. Who you are
56 and what you would are out of my welkin; I might say
    'element,' but the word is over-worn.   *Exit.*

VIOLA
    This fellow is wise enough to play the fool,
59 And to do that well craves a kind of wit.
    He must observe their mood on whom he jests,
    The quality of persons, and the time;
62 And like the haggard, check at every feather
63 That comes before his eye. This is a practice
    As full of labor as a wise man's art;
    For folly that he wisely shows, is fit;
66 But wise men, folly-fall'n, quite taint their wit.
        Enter Sir Toby and [Sir] Andrew.

TOBY Save you, gentleman.

VIOLA And you, sir.

69 ANDREW Dieu vous garde, monsieur.

VIOLA Et vous aussi; votre serviteur.

ANDREW I hope, sir, you are, and I am yours.

72 TOBY Will you encounter the house? My niece is desir-
    ous you should enter, if your trade be to her.

74 VIOLA I am bound to your niece, sir; I mean, she is the list
    of my voyage.

76 TOBY Taste your legs, sir; put them to motion.

77 VIOLA My legs do better understand me, sir, than I under-
    stand what you mean by bidding me taste my legs.

TOBY I mean, to go, sir, to enter.

VIOLA I will answer you with gait and entrance. But we
81 are prevented.
        Enter Olivia and Gentlewoman [Maria].

---

55 *conster* construe, explain **56** *welkin* sky **59** *wit* intelligence **62**
haggard untrained hawk; *check . . . feather* forsake her quarry for other
game **63** *practice* skill **66** *folly-fall'n* fallen into folly; *taint their wit* ruin
their reputation for intelligence **69–70** *Dieu . . . serviteur* God protect
you, sir . . . And you also; your servant **72** *encounter* meet, i.e. go into
74 *bound to* bound for; *list* limit, destination **76** *Taste* try **77** *understand*
both 'comprehend' and 'stand under' **81** *prevented* anticipated

Most excellent accomplished lady, the heavens rain
odors on you.

ANDREW That youth 's a rare courtier. 'Rain odors' –
well!

VIOLA My matter hath no voice, lady, but to your own 85
most pregnant and vouchsafed ear. 86

ANDREW 'Odors,' 'pregnant,' and 'vouchsafed' – I'll get
'em all three all ready.

OLIVIA Let the garden door be shut, and leave me to my
hearing. *[Exeunt Sir Toby, Sir Andrew, and Maria.]*
Give me your hand, sir.

VIOLA
My duty, madam, and most humble service.

OLIVIA
What is your name?

VIOLA
Cesario is your servant's name, fair princess.

OLIVIA
My servant, sir? 'Twas never merry world
Since lowly feigning was called compliment. 96
Y' are servant to the Count Orsino, youth.

VIOLA
And he is yours, and his must needs be yours.
Your servant's servant is your servant, madam.

OLIVIA
For him, I think not on him; for his thoughts,
Would they were blanks, rather than filled with me.

VIOLA
Madam, I come to whet your gentle thoughts
On his behalf.

OLIVIA   O, by your leave, I pray you.
I bade you never speak again of him;
But, would you undertake another suit,
I had rather hear you to solicit that

85 *hath no voice* can be told to no one   86 *pregnant* receptive   96 *lowly
feigning* false humility

107   Than music from the spheres.
    VIOLA   Dear lady –
    OLIVIA
        Give me leave, beseech you. I did send,
        After the last enchantment you did here,
110   A ring in chase of you. So did I abuse
        Myself, my servant, and, I fear me, you.
112   Under your hard construction must I sit,
        To force that on you in a shameful cunning
        Which you knew none of yours. What might you think?
        Have you not set mine honor at the stake
116   And baited it with all th' unmuzzled thoughts
117   That tyrannous heart can think? To one of your
           receiving
118   Enough is shown; a cypress, not a bosom,
        Hides my heart. So, let me hear you speak.
    VIOLA
        I pity you.
    OLIVIA   That's a degree to love.
    VIOLA
121   No, not a grize; for 'tis a vulgar proof
        That very oft we pity enemies.
    OLIVIA
        Why then, methinks 'tis time to smile again.
        O world, how apt the poor are to be proud.
        If one should be a prey, how much the better
        To fall before the lion than the wolf.
           Clock strikes.
        The clock upbraids me with the waste of time.
        Be not afraid, good youth, I will not have you,
        And yet, when wit and youth is come to harvest,
130   Your wife is like to reap a proper man.

---

107 *spheres* the several concentric revolving spheres in which the planets and stars were thought to be placed **110** *abuse* deceive **112** *construction* interpretation **116** *baited* harassed, as a bear by dogs **117** *receiving* receptive capacity **118** *cypress* transparent black cloth **121** *grize* grece, flight of steps; *vulgar proof* common experience **130** *proper* handsome

There lies your way, due west.

VIOLA   Then westward ho!
  Grace and good disposition attend your ladyship.
  You'll nothing, madam, to my lord by me?

OLIVIA
  Stay.
  I prithee tell me what thou think'st of me.

VIOLA
  That you do think you are not what you are.

OLIVIA
  If I think so, I think the same of you.

VIOLA
  Then think you right. I am not what I am.

OLIVIA
  I would you were as I would have you be.

VIOLA
  Would it be better, madam, than I am?
  I wish it might, for now I am your fool.   141

OLIVIA
  O, what a deal of scorn looks beautiful
  In the contempt and anger of his lip.
  A murd'rous guilt shows not itself more soon
  Than love that would seem hid: love's night is noon.
  Cesario, by the roses of the spring,
  By maidhood, honor, truth, and everything,
  I love thee so that, maugre all thy pride,   148
  Nor wit nor reason can my passion hide.
  Do not extort thy reasons from this clause,
  For that I woo, thou therefore hast no cause;
  But rather reason thus with reason fetter,
  Love sought is good, but given unsought is better.

VIOLA
  By innocence I swear, and by my youth,
  I have one heart, one bosom, and one truth,
  And that no woman has; nor never none

141 *fool* butt   **148** *maugre* despite

73

Shall mistress be of it, save I alone.
And so adieu, good madam. Never more
Will I my master's tears to you deplore.

OLIVIA
Yet come again ; for thou perhaps mayst move
That heart which now abhors to like his love.   *Exeunt.*

*

III, ii   *Enter Sir Toby, Sir Andrew, and Fabian.*
ANDREW No, faith, I'll not stay a jot longer.
2 TOBY Thy reason, dear venom ; give thy reason.
FABIAN You must needs yield your reason, Sir Andrew.
ANDREW Marry, I saw your niece do more favors to the
   Count's servingman than ever she bestowed upon me. I
6 saw't i' th' orchard.
TOBY Did she see thee the while, old boy ? Tell me that.
ANDREW As plain as I see you now.
9 FABIAN This was a great argument of love in her toward
   you.
ANDREW 'Slight ! will you make an ass o' me ?
12 FABIAN I will prove it legitimate, sir, upon the oaths of
   judgment and reason.
TOBY And they have been grand-jurymen since before
   Noah was a sailor.
FABIAN She did show favor to the youth in your sight only
17 to exasperate you, to awake your dormouse valor, to put
   fire in your heart and brimstone in your liver. You
   should then have accosted her, and with some excellent
   jests, fire-new from the mint, you should have banged
   the youth into dumbness. This was looked for at your
22 hand, and this was balked. The double gilt of this opportunity you let time wash off, and you are now sailed

---

III, ii Within the house of Olivia 2 *venom* (Sir Andrew is filled with
venom) 6 *orchard* probably 'garden' 9 *argument* proof 12 *legitimate*
true; *oaths* testimony 17 *dormouse* i.e. sleepy 22 *balked* missed; *double
gilt* twice dipped in gold

into the North of my lady's opinion, where you will hang 24
like an icicle on a Dutchman's beard unless you do redeem it by some laudable attempt either of valor or
policy.

ANDREW An't be any way, it must be with valor; for
policy I hate. I had as lief be a Brownist as a politician. 28

TOBY Why then, build me thy fortunes upon the basis of
valor. Challenge me the Count's youth to fight with
him; hurt him in eleven places. My niece shall take note
of it, and assure thyself there is no love-broker in the
world can more prevail in man's commendation with
woman than report of valor.

FABIAN There is no way but this, Sir Andrew.

ANDREW Will either of you bear me a challenge to him?

TOBY Go, write it in a martial hand. Be curst and brief; it 37
is no matter how witty, so it be eloquent and full of invention. Taunt him with the license of ink. If thou thou'st 39
him some thrice, it shall not be amiss; and as many lies as
will lie in thy sheet of paper, although the sheet were big
enough for the bed of Ware in England, set 'em down. 42
Go about it. Let there be gall enough in thy ink, though
thou write with a goose-pen, no matter. About it!

ANDREW Where shall I find you?

TOBY We'll call thee at the cubiculo. Go. 46

Exit Sir Andrew.

FABIAN This is a dear manikin to you, Sir Toby. 47

TOBY I have been dear to him, lad, some two thousand
strong or so.

FABIAN We shall have a rare letter from him, but you'll
not deliver't?

TOBY Never trust me then; and by all means stir on the
youth to an answer. I think oxen and wainropes cannot 53

24 *into the North* i.e. out of the warmth   28 *Brownist* early Congregationalist
37 *curst* perversely cross   39 *license of ink* i.e. unrestrained writing   39–40
thou'st him call him 'thou' instead of the polite 'you'   42 *bed of Ware* a
famous bed, over ten feet wide   46 *cubiculo* little chamber   47 *manikin*
puppet   53 *wainropes* wagon ropes

54   hale them together. For Andrew, if he were opened, and
       you find so much blood in his liver as will clog the foot of
       a flea, I'll eat the rest of th' anatomy.

   FABIAN And his opposite, the youth, bears in his visage
       no great presage of cruelty.
           Enter Maria.
59 TOBY Look where the youngest wren of mine comes.
60 MARIA If you desire the spleen, and will laugh yourselves
61   into stitches, follow me. Yond gull Malvolio is turned
       heathen, a very renegado; for there is no Christian that
       means to be saved by believing rightly can ever believe
64   such impossible passages of grossness. He's in yellow
       stockings.
   TOBY And cross-gartered?
   MARIA Most villainously; like a pedant that keeps a school
       i' th' church. I have dogged him like his murderer. He
       does obey every point of the letter that I dropped to be-
       tray him. He does smile his face into more lines than is
71   in the new map with the augmentation of the Indies.
       You have not seen such a thing as 'tis. I can hardly for-
       bear hurling things at him. I know my lady will strike
       him. If she do, he'll smile, and take't for a great favor.
   TOBY Come bring us, bring us where he is.
                                        Exeunt omnes.

                           *

III, iii   *Enter Sebastian and Antonio.*
   SEBASTIAN
       I would not by my will have troubled you;
       But since you make your pleasure of your pains,
       I will no further chide you.

---

54 *hale* haul   59 *youngest wren* smallest of small birds   60 *spleen* a laughing
fit   61 *gull* dupe   64 *passages of grossness* statements of exaggerated
misinformation   71 *map . . . Indies* (Emerie Molyneux's map, ca. 1599,
which gave fuller details of the East Indies and North America, with
meridian lines, etc.)
III, iii A street in the Illyrian capital

ANTONIO

    I could not stay behind you. My desire
    (More sharp than filèd steel) did spur me forth;
    And not all love to see you (though so much   6
    As might have drawn one to a longer voyage)
    But jealousy what might befall your travel,   8
    Being skilless in these parts; which to a stranger,   9
    Unguided and unfriended, often prove
    Rough and unhospitable. My willing love,
    The rather by these arguments of fear,
    Set forth in your pursuit.

SEBASTIAN   My kind Antonio,
    I can no other answer make but thanks,
    And thanks, and ever oft good turns
    Are shuffled off with such uncurrent pay.   16
    But, were my worth as is my conscience firm,   17
    You should find better dealing. What's to do?
    Shall we go see the relics of this town?   19

ANTONIO

    To-morrow, sir; best first go see your lodging.

SEBASTIAN

    I am not weary, and 'tis long to night.
    I pray you let us satisfy our eyes
    With the memorials and the things of fame
    That do renown this city.

ANTONIO   Would you'ld pardon me.
    I do not without danger walk these streets.
    Once in a sea-fight 'gainst the Count his galleys
    I did some service; of such note indeed
    That, were I ta'en here, it would scarce be answered.   28

SEBASTIAN

    Belike you slew great number of his people?

ANTONIO

    Th' offense is not of such a bloody nature,

---

6 *not all* not only, not entirely   8 *jealousy* solicitude   9 *skilless in* without
knowledge of   16 *uncurrent* valueless   17 *worth* wealth; *conscience* right
inclination   19 *relics* monuments   28 *answered* atoned for

Albeit the quality of the time and quarrel
Might well have given us bloody argument.
It might have since been answered in repaying
34   What we took from them, which for traffic's sake
Most of our city did. Only myself stood out;
36   For which, if I be lapsèd in this place,
I shall pay dear.

SEBASTIAN   Do not then walk too open.

ANTONIO
It doth not fit me. Hold, sir, here's my purse.
39   In the south suburbs at the Elephant
Is best to lodge. I will bespeak our diet,
Whiles you beguile the time and feed your knowledge
With viewing of the town. There shall you have me.

SEBASTIAN
Why I your purse?

ANTONIO
44   Haply your eye shall light upon some toy
45   You have desire to purchase, and your store
46   I think is not for idle markets, sir.

SEBASTIAN
I'll be your purse-bearer, and leave you for
An hour.

ANTONIO To th' Elephant.

SEBASTIAN   I do remember.   *Exeunt.*

*

III, iv   *Enter Olivia and Maria.*

OLIVIA
I have sent after him; he says he'll come.
2   How shall I feast him? What bestow of him?
For youth is bought more oft than begged or borrowed.

---

34 *traffic's* trade's 36 *lapsèd* surprised, pounced upon 39 *the Elephant*
an inn 44 *toy* trifle 45 *store* store of money 46 *idle markets* useless
purchasings
III, iv The garden of Olivia's house 2 *of* on

I speak too loud. Where's Malvolio? He is sad and civil, 4
And suits well for a servant with my fortunes.
Where is Malvolio?

MARIA He's coming, madam, but in very strange manner.
He is sure possessed, madam. 8

OLIVIA Why, what's the matter? Does he rave?

MARIA No, madam, he does nothing but smile. Your
ladyship were best to have some guard about you if he
come, for sure the man is tainted in 's wits.

OLIVIA
Go call him hither. I am as mad as he,
If sad and merry madness equal be.
       Enter Malvolio.
How now, Malvolio?

MALVOLIO Sweet lady, ho, ho!

OLIVIA Smil'st thou? I sent for thee upon a sad occasion.

MALVOLIO Sad, lady? I could be sad. This does make
some obstruction in the blood, this cross-gartering; but
what of that? If it please the eye of one, it is with me as
the very true sonnet is, 'Please one, and please all.' 21

OLIVIA Why, how dost thou, man? What is the matter
with thee?

MALVOLIO Not black in my mind, though yellow in my
legs. It did come to his hands, and commands shall be
executed. I think we do know the sweet Roman hand. 26

OLIVIA Wilt thou go to bed, Malvolio?

MALVOLIO To bed? Ay, sweetheart, and I'll come to
thee.

OLIVIA God comfort thee. Why dost thou smile so, and
kiss thy hand so oft?

MARIA How do you, Malvolio?

MALVOLIO At your request? Yes, nightingales answer
daws! 32

MARIA Why appear you with this ridiculous boldness before my lady?

---

4 *sad and civil* serious and sedate   8 *possessed* mad   21 *sonnet* any short
poem   26 *Roman hand* Italian style of handwriting   32 *daws* small crows

79

MALVOLIO 'Be not afraid of greatness.' 'Twas well writ.

OLIVIA What mean'st thou by that, Malvolio?

MALVOLIO 'Some are born great.'

OLIVIA Ha?

MALVOLIO 'Some achieve greatness.'

40 OLIVIA What say'st thou?

MALVOLIO 'And some have greatness thrust upon them.'

OLIVIA Heaven restore thee!

MALVOLIO 'Remember who commended thy yellow
stockings.'

OLIVIA Thy yellow stockings?

MALVOLIO 'And wished to see thee cross-gartered.'

OLIVIA Cross-gartered?

MALVOLIO 'Go to, thou art made, if thou desir'st to be
so.'

OLIVIA Am I made?

MALVOLIO 'If not, let me see thee a servant still.'

OLIVIA Why, this is very midsummer madness.

    Enter Servant.

SERVANT Madam, the young gentleman of the Count
Orsino's is returned. I could hardly entreat him back.
He attends your ladyship's pleasure.

OLIVIA I'll come to him. *[Exit Servant.]* Good Maria, let
this fellow be looked to. Where's my cousin Toby? Let
some of my people have a special care of him. I would
58   not have him miscarry for the half of my dowry.

                Exit [Olivia; then Maria].

MALVOLIO O ho, do you come near me now? No worse
man than Sir Toby to look to me. This concurs directly
with the letter. She sends him on purpose, that I may
62   appear stubborn to him; for she incites me to that in the
letter. 'Cast thy humble slough,' says she; 'be opposite
with a kinsman, surly with servants; let thy tongue tang
with arguments of state; put thyself into the trick of singularity.' And consequently sets down the manner how:

---

58 *miscarry* come to harm   62 *stubborn* hard, stiff, rigid

as, a sad face, a reverend carriage, a slow tongue, in the
habit of some sir of note, and so forth. I have limed her; 68
but it is Jove's doing, and Jove make me thankful. And
when she went away now, 'Let this fellow be looked to.'
'Fellow.' Not 'Malvolio,' nor after my degree, but 'fel- 71
low.' Why, everything adheres together, that no dram of 72
a scruple, no scruple of a scruple, no obstacle, no in- 73
credulous or unsafe circumstance – what can be said?
Nothing that can be can come between me and the full
prospect of my hopes. Well, Jove, not I, is the doer of
this, and he is to be thanked.

    Enter [Sir] Toby, Fabian, and Maria.

TOBY Which way is he, in the name of sanctity? If all the
devils of hell be drawn in little, and Legion himself pos- 79
sessed him, yet I'll speak to him.

FABIAN Here he is, here he is! How is't with you, sir?

TOBY How is't with you, man?

MALVOLIO Go off; I discard you. Let me enjoy my
private. Go off.

MARIA Lo, how hollow the fiend speaks within him!
Did not I tell you? Sir Toby, my lady prays you to have
a care of him.

MALVOLIO Aha! does she so?

TOBY Go to, go to; peace, peace; we must deal gently
with him. Let me alone. How do you, Malvolio? How
is't with you? What, man, defy the devil? Consider,
he's an enemy to mankind.

MALVOLIO Do you know what you say?

MARIA La you, an you speak ill of the devil, how he takes
it at heart. Pray God he be not bewitched.

FABIAN Carry his water to th' wise woman. 96

MARIA Marry, and it shall be done to-morrow morning if

---

68 *limed* caught   **71** *Fellow* companion; *after my degree* according to my
position   **72** *dram* (1) small bit, (2) one-eighth fluid ounce   **73** *scruple* (1)
doubt, (2) one-third of a dram; *incredulous* incredible   **79** *drawn in little*
brought together in a small space; *Legion* troop of fiends   **96** *water* urine
for medical analysis; *wise woman* herb woman

I live. My lady would not lose him for more than I'll say.

MALVOLIO How now, mistress?

MARIA O Lord.

TOBY Prithee hold thy peace. This is not the way. Do you
102 not see you move him? Let me alone with him.

FABIAN No way but gentleness; gently, gently. The fiend
is rough and will not be roughly used.

105 TOBY Why, how now, my bawcock? How dost thou,
106 chuck?

MALVOLIO Sir.

108 TOBY Ay, biddy, come with me. What, man, 'tis not for
109 gravity to play at cherry-pit with Satan. Hang him, foul
110 collier!

MARIA Get him to say his prayers; good Sir Toby, get
him to pray.

MALVOLIO My prayers, minx?

MARIA No, I warrant you, he will not hear of godliness.

115 MALVOLIO Go hang yourselves all! You are idle shallow
things; I am not of your element. You shall know more
hereafter.   *Exit.*

TOBY Is't possible?

FABIAN If this were played upon a stage now, I could
condemn it as an improbable fiction.

121 TOBY His very genius hath taken the infection of the device, man.

123 MARIA Nay, pursue him now, lest the device take air and
taint.

FABIAN Why, we shall make him mad indeed.

MARIA The house will be the quieter.

TOBY Come, we'll have him in a dark room and bound.
My niece is already in the belief that he's mad. We may
129 carry it thus, for our pleasure and his penance, till our

102 *move* rouse   105 *bawcock* fine fellow (French '*beau coq*')   106 *chuck*
chick   108 *biddy* chicken   109 *gravity* dignity; *cherry-pit* a child's game
110 *collier* coal peddler (Satan)   115 *idle* empty, trifling   121 *genius*
nature   124–24 *take air and taint* be exposed and thus contaminated   129
carry it carry the trick on

very pastime, tired out of breath, prompt us to have
mercy on him; at which time we will bring the device to
the bar and crown thee for a finder of madmen. But see,
but see.

Enter Sir Andrew.

FABIAN More matter for a May morning.   134

ANDREW Here's the challenge; read it. I warrant there's
vinegar and pepper in't.

FABIAN Is't so saucy?   137

ANDREW Ay, is't, I warrant him. Do but read.

TOBY Give me. *[reads]* 'Youth, whatsoever thou art, thou
art but a scurvy fellow.'

FABIAN Good, and valiant.

TOBY *[reads]* 'Wonder not nor admire not in thy mind   142
why I do call thee so, for I will show thee no reason for't.'

FABIAN A good note that keeps you from the blow of the
law.

TOBY *[reads]* 'Thou com'st to the Lady Olivia, and in my
sight she uses thee kindly. But thou liest in thy throat;
that is not the matter I challenge thee for.'

FABIAN Very brief, and to exceeding good sense – less.

TOBY *[reads]* 'I will waylay thee going home; where if it
be thy chance to kill me' –

FABIAN Good.

TOBY *[reads]* 'Thou kill'st me like a rogue and a villain.'

FABIAN Still you keep o' th' windy side of the law. Good.   154

TOBY *[reads]* 'Fare thee well, and God have mercy upon
one of our souls. He may have mercy upon mine, but my
hope is better, and so look to thyself. Thy friend, as thou
usest him, and thy sworn enemy,

                                  'Andrew Aguecheek.'

If this letter move him not, his legs cannot. I'll give't
him.

MARIA You may have very fit occasion for't. He is now in
some commerce with my lady and will by and by depart.

134 *matter . . . morning* material for a May-day comedy   137 *saucy* (1) spicy,
(2) impudent, sharp   142 *admire* be amazed   154 *windy* windward, safe

TOBY Go, Sir Andrew. Scout me for him at the corner of
164   the orchard like a bum-baily. So soon as ever thou seest
          him, draw; and as thou draw'st, swear horrible; for it
          comes to pass oft that a terrible oath, with a swaggering
167   accent sharply twanged off, gives manhood more appro-
168   bation than ever proof itself would have earned him.
          Away!
170 ANDREW Nay, let me alone for swearing.   *Exit.*
     TOBY Now will not I deliver his letter; for the behavior of
          the young gentleman gives him out to be of good capaci-
          ty and breeding; his employment between his lord and
          my niece confirms no less. Therefore this letter, being so
          excellently ignorant, will breed no terror in the youth.
          He will find it comes from a clodpoll. But, sir, I will de-
          liver his challenge by word of mouth, set upon Ague-
          cheek a notable report of valor, and drive the gentleman
          (as I know his youth will aptly receive it) into a most
          hideous opinion of his rage, skill, fury, and impetuosity.
          This will so fright them both that they will kill one
182   another by the look, like cockatrices.
               Enter Olivia and Viola.
     FABIAN Here he comes with your niece. Give them way
          till he take leave, and presently after him.
     TOBY I will meditate the while upon some horrid mes-
          sage for a challenge.
                    [Exeunt Sir Toby, Fabian, and Maria.]
     OLIVIA
          I have said too much unto a heart of stone
188   And laid mine honor too unchary on't.
          There's something in me that reproves my fault;
          But such a headstrong potent fault it is
          That it but mocks reproof.

---

164 *bum-baily* an agent employed in making arrests **167** *manhood more
approbation* more reputation for courage **168** *proof* testing **170** *let . . .
swearing* leave swearing to me **182** *cockatrices* basilisks, reptiles able to kill
with a glance **188** *unchary on't* carelessly on it (the heart of stone)

VIOLA

   With the same havior that your passion bears   192
   Goes on my master's griefs.

OLIVIA

   Here, wear this jewel for me ; 'tis my picture.   194
   Refuse it not ; it hath no tongue to vex you.
   And I beseech you come again to-morrow.
   What shall you ask of me that I'll deny,
   That honor, saved, may upon asking give ?

VIOLA

   Nothing but this : your true love for my master.

OLIVIA

   How with mine honor may I give him that
   Which I have given to you ?

VIOLA   I will acquit you.

OLIVIA

   Well, come again to-morrow. Fare thee well.
   A fiend like thee might bear my soul to hell.   *[Exit.]* 203
      Enter [Sir] Toby and Fabian.

TOBY Gentleman, God save thee.

VIOLA And you, sir.

TOBY That defense thou hast, betake thee to't. Of what
   nature the wrongs are thou hast done him, I know not ;
   but thy intercepter, full of despite, bloody as the hunter, 208
   attends thee at the orchard end. Dismount thy tuck, be 209
   yare in thy preparation, for thy assailant is quick, skill- 210
   ful, and deadly.

VIOLA You mistake, sir. I am sure no man hath any quarrel to me. My remembrance is very free and clear from
   any image of offense done to any man.

TOBY You'll find it otherwise, I assure you. Therefore, if
   you hold your life at any price, betake you to your guard ;
   for your opposite hath in him what youth, strength,
   skill, and wrath can furnish man withal.

---

192 *havior* behavior **194** *jewel* any ornament or trinket; here perhaps
'locket' **203** *like thee* in your likeness **208** *despite* defiance **209** *Dismount thy tuck* take out your rapier **210** *yare* quick

VIOLA I pray you, sir, what is he?

220 TOBY He is knight, dubbed with unhatched rapier and on
carpet consideration, but he is a devil in private brawl.
Souls and bodies hath he divorced three; and his in-
censement at this moment is so implacable that satis-
faction can be none but by pangs of death and sepulchre.

225 'Hob, nob' is his word; 'give't or take't.'

VIOLA I will return again into the house and desire some
227 conduct of the lady. I am no fighter. I have heard of
some kind of men that put quarrels purposely on others
229 to taste their valor. Belike this is a man of that quirk.

TOBY Sir, no. His indignation derives itself out of a very
231 competent injury; therefore get you on and give him his
desire. Back you shall not to the house, unless you undertake that with me which with as much safety you might
answer him. Therefore on, or strip your sword stark
235 naked; for meddle you must, that's certain, or forswear
to wear iron about you.

VIOLA This is as uncivil as strange. I beseech you do me
this courteous office, as to know of the knight what my
offense to him is. It is something of my negligence,
nothing of my purpose.

TOBY I will do so. Signior Fabian, stay you by this gentleman till my return.   *Exit.*

VIOLA Pray you, sir, do you know of this matter?

FABIAN I know the knight is incensed against you, even
245 to a mortal arbitrement; but nothing of the circumstance more.

VIOLA I beseech you, what manner of man is he?

FABIAN Nothing of that wonderful promise, to read him
by his form, as you are like to find him in the proof of his

---

220 *unhatched* unhacked 220-21 *on carpet consideration* through court
favor 225 *Hob, nob* have or have not 227 *conduct* protective escort
229 *taste* test; *quirk* peculiarity 231 *competent* sufficient 235 *meddle*
engage (in the fight) 235-36 *forswear . . . iron* repudiate on oath (your
right) to wear a sword 245 *mortal arbitrement* deadly settlement

valor. He is indeed, sir, the most skillful, bloody, and
fatal opposite that you could possibly have found in any
part of Illyria. Will you walk towards him? I will make
your peace with him if I can.

VIOLA I shall be much bound to you for't. I am one that
had rather go with sir priest than sir knight. I care not
who knows so much of my mettle.   *Exeunt.*
      Enter [Sir] Toby and [Sir] Andrew.

TOBY Why, man, he's a very devil; I have not seen such a
firago. I had a pass with him, rapier, scabbard, and all, 258
and he gives me the stuck-in with such a mortal motion 259
that it is inevitable; and on the answer he pays you as 260
surely as your feet hits the ground they step on. They
say he has been fencer to the Sophy.

ANDREW Pox on't, I'll not meddle with him.

TOBY Ay, but he will not now be pacified. Fabian can
scarce hold him yonder.

ANDREW Plague on't, an I thought he had been valiant,
and so cunning in fence. I'd have seen him damned ere
I'd have challenged him. Let him let the matter slip, and
I'll give him my horse, grey Capilet.

TOBY I'll make the motion. Stand here; make a good 270
show on't. This shall end without the perdition of souls. 271
[aside] Marry, I'll ride your horse as well as I ride you.
      Enter Fabian and Viola.
I have his horse to take up the quarrel. I have persuaded 273
him the youth's a devil.

FABIAN He is as horribly conceited of him, and pants and 275
looks pale, as if a bear were at his heels.

TOBY There's no remedy, sir; he will fight with you for's
oath sake. Marry, he hath better bethought him of his
quarrel, and he finds that now scarce to be worth talking

---

258 *firago* virago; *pass* bout   259 *stuck-in* thrust, lunge; *motion* action
260 *answer* return   270 *motion* offer   271 *the perdition of souls* i.e. killing
273 *take up* settle   275 *He . . . him* he (Cesario) has just as frightening a
conception of him (Sir Andrew)

of. Therefore draw for the supportance of his vow. He
protests he will not hurt you.

VIOLA *[aside]* Pray God defend me! A little thing would
make me tell them how much I lack of a man.

FABIAN Give ground if you see him furious.

TOBY Come, Sir Andrew, there's no remedy. The gentleman will for his honor's sake have one bout with you; he
287 cannot by the duello avoid it; but he has promised me,
as he is a gentleman and a soldier, he will not hurt you.
Come on, to't.

ANDREW Pray God he keep his oath!
    [Draws.]
    Enter Antonio.

VIOLA
I do assure you 'tis against my will.
    [Draws.]

ANTONIO
Put up your sword. If this young gentleman
Have done offense, I take the fault on me;
If you offend him, I for him defy you.

TOBY You, sir? Why, what are you?

ANTONIO *[draws]*
One, sir, that for his love dares yet do more
Than you have heard him brag to you he will.

298 TOBY Nay, if you be an undertaker, I am for you.
    [Draws.]
    Enter Officers.

FABIAN O good Sir Toby, hold. Here come the officers.

TOBY *[to Antonio]* I'll be with you anon.

VIOLA *[to Sir Andrew]* Pray, sir, put your sword up, if
you please.

ANDREW Marry, will I, sir; and for that I promised you,
I'll be as good as my word. He will bear you easily, and
reins well.

1. OFFICER This is the man; do thy office.

---

287 *duello* duelling code   **298** *undertaker* one who takes up a challenge

2. OFFICER
Antonio, I arrest thee at the suit
Of Count Orsino.
ANTONIO   You do mistake me, sir.
1. OFFICER
No, sir, no jot. I know your favor well,   309
Though now you have no sea-cap on your head.
Take him away. He knows I know him well.
ANTONIO
I must obey. *[to Viola]* This comes with seeking you.
But there's no remedy; I shall answer it.
What will you do, now my necessity
Makes me to ask you for my purse? It grieves me
Much more for what I cannot do for you
Than what befalls myself. You stand amazed,
But be of comfort
2. OFFICER Come, sir, away.
ANTONIO
I must entreat of you some of that money.
VIOLA
What money, sir?
For the fair kindness you have showed me here,
And part being prompted by your present trouble,
Out of my lean and low ability
I'll lend you something. My having is not much.
I'll make division of my present with you.   326
Hold, there's half my coffer.   327
ANTONIO   Will you deny me now?
Is't possible that my deserts to you
Can lack persuasion? Do not tempt my misery,
Lest that it make me so unsound a man
As to upbraid you with those kindnesses
That I have done for you.
VIOLA   I know of none,
Nor know I you by voice or any feature.

309 *favor* face   326 *my present* what I have now   327 *coffer* money

89

I hate ingratitude more in a man
Than lying, vainness, babbling, drunkenness,
Or any taint of vice whose strong corruption
Inhabits our frail blood.

ANTONIO   O heavens themselves!

2. OFFICER
Come, sir, I pray you go.

ANTONIO
Let me speak a little. This youth that you see here
I snatched one half out of the jaws of death;
Relieved him with such sanctity of love,
And to his image, which methought did promise
343 Most venerable worth, did I devotion.

1. OFFICER
What's that to us? The time goes by. Away.

ANTONIO
But, O, how vile an idol proves this god!
Thou hast, Sebastian, done good feature shame.
In nature there's no blemish but the mind;
348 None can be called deformed but the unkind.
349 Virtue is beauty; but the beauteous evil
350 Are empty trunks, o'erflourished by the devil.

1. OFFICER
The man grows mad; away with him! Come, come, sir.

ANTONIO Lead me on.   Exit [with Officers].

VIOLA
Methinks his words do from such passion fly
That he believes himself; so do not I.
Prove true, imagination, O, prove true,
That I, dear brother, be now ta'en for you!

TOBY Come hither, knight; come hither, Fabian. We'll
358 whisper o'er a couplet or two of most sage saws.

VIOLA
He named Sebastian. I my brother know

343 *venerable* worthy of veneration   348 *unkind* unnatural   349 *beauteous* fair-seeming   350 *trunks* chests; *o'erflourished* ornamented   358 *sage saws* wise sayings

Yet living in my glass. Even such and so   360
In favor was my brother, and he went
Still in this fashion, color, ornament,
For him I imitate. O, if it prove,
Tempests are kind, and salt waves fresh in love! *[Exit.]*

TOBY A very dishonest paltry boy, and more a coward 365
than a hare. His dishonesty appears in leaving his friend
here in necessity and denying him; and for his coward-
ship, ask Fabian.

FABIAN A coward, a most devout coward; religious in it. 369

ANDREW 'Slid, I'll after him again and beat him.

TOBY Do; cuff him soundly, but never draw thy sword.

ANDREW An I do not –   *[Exit.]*

FABIAN Come, let's see the event.   373

TOBY I dare lay any money 'twill be nothing yet. *Exeunt.* 374

*

Enter Sebastian and Clown.   IV, i

CLOWN Will you make me believe that I am not sent for
you?

SEBASTIAN Go to, go to, thou art a foolish fellow. Let me
be clear of thee.

CLOWN Well held out, i' faith! No, I do not know you; 5
nor I am not sent to you by my lady, to bid you come
speak with her; nor your name is not Master Cesario;
nor this is not my nose neither. Nothing that is so is so.

SEBASTIAN I prithee vent thy folly somewhere else.
Thou know'st not me.

CLOWN Vent my folly! He has heard that word of some
great man, and now applies it to a fool. Vent my folly!
I am afraid this great lubber, the world, will prove a 13
cockney. I prithee now, ungird thy strangeness, and tell 14

___

360 *Yet . . . glass* i.e. whenever I look in the mirror   365 *dishonest* dishonorable   369 *religious* confirmed   373 *event* result   374 *yet* nevertheless
IV, i Before Olivia's house   5 *held out* kept up   13 *lubber* lout   14 *cockney*
affected person; *ungird thy strangeness* abandon your strange manner

me what I shall vent to my lady. Shall I vent to her that
thou art coming?

17 SEBASTIAN I prithee, foolish Greek, depart from me.
There's money for thee. If you tarry longer, I shall give
worse payment.

CLOWN By my troth, thou hast an open hand. These wise
men that give fools money get themselves a good report
22 – after fourteen years' purchase.

Enter [Sir] Andrew, [Sir] Toby, and Fabian.

ANDREW Now, sir, have I met you again? There's for
you!
[Strikes Sebastian.]

SEBASTIAN Why, there's for thee, and there, and there!
[Strikes Sir Andrew.]
Are all the people mad?

TOBY Hold, sir, or I'll throw your dagger o'er the house.
[Seizes Sebastian.]

CLOWN This will I tell my lady straight. I would not be in
some of your coats for two-pence.   *Exit.*

TOBY Come on, sir; hold.

ANDREW Nay, let him alone. I'll go another way to work
31 with him. I'll have an action of battery against him, if
there be any law in Illyria. Though I struck him first,
yet it's no matter for that.

SEBASTIAN Let go thy hand.

TOBY Come, sir, I will not let you go. Come, my young
36 soldier, put up your iron. You are well fleshed. Come on.

SEBASTIAN
I will be free from thee.
[Frees himself.]   What wouldst thou now?
If thou dar'st tempt me further, draw thy sword.
[Draws.]

TOBY What, what? Nay then, I must have an ounce or
40 two of this malapert blood from you.

17 *Greek* merry companion   22 *after . . . purchase* i.e. at a high price   31
action of battery suit at law for beating (me)   36 *well fleshed* made fierce by
a taste of blood   40 *malapert* impudent

[Draws.]
Enter Olivia.

OLIVIA

Hold, Toby! On thy life I charge thee hold!

TOBY Madam.

OLIVIA

Will it be ever thus? Ungracious wretch,
Fit for the mountains and the barbarous caves,
Where manners ne'er were preached! Out of my sight!
Be not offended, dear Cesario.
Rudesby, be gone.   47
                [Exeunt Sir Toby, Sir Andrew, and Fabian.]
                        I prithee, gentle friend,
Let thy fair wisdom, not thy passion, sway
In this uncivil and unjust extent   49
Against thy peace. Go with me to my house,
And hear thou there how many fruitless pranks
This ruffian hath botched up, that thou thereby   52
Mayst smile at this. Thou shalt not choose but go.
Do not deny. Beshrew his soul for me.   54
He started one poor heart of mine, in thee.   55

SEBASTIAN

What relish is in this? How runs the stream?   56
Or I am mad, or else this is a dream.
Let fancy still my sense in Lethe steep;   58
If it be thus to dream, still let me sleep!

OLIVIA

Nay, come, I prithee. Would thou'dst be ruled by me!

SEBASTIAN

Madam, I will.

OLIVIA   O, say so, and so be.   *Exeunt.*

*

47 *Rudesby* unmannerly fellow 49 *uncivil* uncivilized; *extent* probably
'display' 52 *botched up* contrived 54 *Beshrew* curse 55 *started* startled;
heart (with a pun on 'hart') 56 *relish* taste 58 *Lethe* the river of forgetful-
ness in the underworld

IV, ii   *Enter Maria and Clown.*

    MARIA Nay, I prithee put on this gown and this beard;
2   make him believe thou art Sir Topas the curate; do it
    quickly. I'll call Sir Toby the whilst.   *[Exit.]*
4   CLOWN Well, I'll put it on, and I will dissemble myself
    in't, and I would I were the first that ever dissembled in
6   such a gown. I am not tall enough to become the function
    well, nor lean enough to be thought a good student; but
8   to be said an honest man and a good housekeeper goes as
    fairly as to say a careful man and a great scholar. The
10   competitors enter.
    Enter [Sir] Toby [and Maria].

    TOBY Jove bless thee, Master Parson.
12   CLOWN Bonos dies, Sir Toby; for, as the old hermit of
    Prague, that never saw pen and ink, very wittily said to a
14   niece of King Gorboduc, 'That that is is'; so, I, being
    Master Parson, am Master Parson; for what is 'that'
    but that, and 'is' but is?

    TOBY To him, Sir Topas.

    CLOWN What ho, I say. Peace in this prison!
19   TOBY The knave counterfeits well; a good knave.
    Malvolio within.

    MALVOLIO Who calls there?

    CLOWN Sir Topas the curate, who comes to visit Mal-
    volio the lunatic.

    MALVOLIO Sir Topas, Sir Topas, good Sir Topas, go to
    my lady.
25   CLOWN Out, hyperbolical fiend! How vexest thou this
    man! Talkest thou nothing but of ladies?

    TOBY Well said, Master Parson.

IV, ii Within Olivia's house   **2** *Sir* (common title of address for the clergy);
Topas (comic knight in Chaucer; the topaz stone was thought to cure
insanity   **4** *dissemble* disguise   **6** *function* function of a cleric   **8** *good
housekeeper* householder, neighbor   **10** *competitors* associates   **12** *Bonos
dies* good day   **12–13** *the old hermit of Prague* (probably the clown's invention)   **14** *King Gorboduc* a legendary British king who appeared in an early
English tragedy   **19** *knave* boy, fellow   **25** *hyperbolical* enormous

MALVOLIO Sir Topas, never was man thus wronged. Good Sir Topas, do not think I am mad. They have laid me here in hideous darkness.

CLOWN Fie, thou dishonest Satan. I call thee by the 31 most modest terms, for I am one of those gentle ones that will use the devil himself with courtesy. Say'st thou that house is dark? 34

MALVOLIO As hell, Sir Topas.

CLOWN Why, it hath bay windows transparent as barri- 36 cadoes, and the clerestories toward the south north are 37 as lustrous as ebony; and yet complainest thou of obstruction?

MALVOLIO I am not mad, Sir Topas. I say to you this house is dark.

CLOWN Madman, thou errest. I say there is no darkness but ignorance, in which thou art more puzzled than the Egyptians in their fog. 44

MALVOLIO I say this house is as dark as ignorance, though ignorance were as dark as hell; and I say there was never man thus abused. I am no more mad than you are. Make the trial of it in any constant question. 48

CLOWN What is the opinion of Pythagoras concerning 49 wild fowl?

MALVOLIO That the soul of our grandam might happily 51 inhabit a bird.

CLOWN What think'st thou of his opinion?

MALVOLIO I think nobly of the soul and no way approve his opinion.

CLOWN Fare thee well. Remain thou still in darkness. Thou shalt hold th' opinion of Pythagoras ere I will allow of thy wits, and fear to kill a woodcock, lest thou 57 dispossess the soul of thy grandam. Fare thee well.

---

31 *dishonest* dishonorable   34 *house* darkened room   36 *barricadoes* barri-
cades   37 *clerestories* upper windows   44 *fog* (Moses brought a three-day
fog on the Egyptians)   48 *constant question* consistent discussion   49
Pythagoras (who originated the doctrine of transmigration of souls)
51 *happily* haply, by chance   57 *allow of* acknowledge

MALVOLIO Sir Topas, Sir Topas!

TOBY My most exquisite Sir Topas!

62 CLOWN Nay, I am for all waters.

MARIA Thou mightest have done this without thy beard
and gown. He sees thee not.

TOBY To him in thine own voice, and bring me word how
thou find'st him. *[to Maria]* I would we were well rid of
this knavery. If he may be conveniently delivered, I
would he were; for I am now so far in offense with my
niece that I cannot pursue with any safety this sport to
70 the upshot. *[to the Clown]* Come by and by to my
chamber.   *Exit [with Maria].*

71 CLOWN *[sings]*   'Hey, Robin, jolly Robin,
                    Tell me how thy lady does.'

MALVOLIO Fool.

74 CLOWN 'My lady is unkind, perdie!'

MALVOLIO Fool.

CLOWN 'Alas, why is she so?'

MALVOLIO Fool, I say.

CLOWN 'She loves another.' Who calls, ha?

MALVOLIO Good fool, as ever thou wilt deserve well at
my hand, help me to a candle, and pen, ink, and paper.
As I am a gentleman, I will live to be thankful to thee
for't.

CLOWN Master Malvolio?

MALVOLIO Ay, good fool.

84 CLOWN Alas, sir, how fell you besides your five wits?

MALVOLIO Fool, there was never man so notoriously
abused. I am as well in my wits, fool, as thou art.

CLOWN But as well? Then you are mad indeed, if you be
no better in your wits than a fool.

89 MALVOLIO They have here propertied me; keep me in

---

62 *for all waters* i.e. good for any trade   70 *upshot* outcome   71 *Hey,
Robin* . . . (from an old song, sometimes attributed to Sir Thomas Wyatt)
74 *perdie* certainly   84 *besides your five wits* out of your mind   89 *propertied
me* made me a property, a mere thing

96

darkness, send ministers to me, asses, and do all they
can to face me out of my wits.   91

CLOWN Advise you what you say. The minister is here. – 92
Malvolio, Malvolio, thy wits the heavens restore. En-
deavor thyself to sleep and leave thy vain bibble babble.

MALVOLIO Sir Topas.

CLOWN Maintain no words with him, good fellow. –
Who, I, sir? Not I, sir. God b' wi' you, good Sir Topas.
– Marry, amen. – I will, sir, I will.

MALVOLIO Fool, fool, fool, I say!

CLOWN Alas, sir, be patient. What say you, sir? I am shent 100
for speaking to you.

MALVOLIO Good fool, help me to some light and some
paper. I tell thee, I am as well in my wits as any man in
Illyria.

CLOWN Well-a-day that you were, sir.   105

MALVOLIO By this hand, I am. Good fool, some ink,
paper, and light; and convey what I will set down to my
lady. It shall advantage thee more than ever the bearing
of letter did.

CLOWN I will help you to't. But tell me true, are you not
mad indeed? or do you but counterfeit?

MALVOLIO Believe me, I am not. I tell thee true.

CLOWN Nay, I'll ne'er believe a madman till I see his
brains. I will fetch you light and paper and ink.

MALVOLIO Fool, I'll requite it in the highest degree. I
prithee be gone.

CLOWN [sings]   I am gone, sir,
                       And anon, sir,
                  I'll be with you again,
                       In a trice,
                       Like to the old Vice,   121
                  Your need to sustain.
                  Who with dagger of lath,

91 *face me* brazen me   92 *Advise you* be careful   100 *shent* reproved   105
Well-a-day woe, alas   121 *Vice* comic character of the morality plays

> In his rage and his wrath,
>> Cries 'Ah ha' to the devil.
> Like a mad lad,
>> 'Pare thy nails, dad.'
>>> Adieu, goodman devil.   *Exit.*

*

IV, iii   *Enter Sebastian.*

SEBASTIAN

This is the air ; that is the glorious sun ;
This pearl she gave me, I do feel't and see't ;
And though 'tis wonder that enwraps me thus,
Yet 'tis not madness. Where's Antonio then ?
I could not find him at the Elephant ;

6   Yet there he was, and there I found this credit,
That he did range the town to seek me out.
His counsel now might do me golden service ;
For though my soul disputes well with my sense
That this may be some error, but no madness,
Yet doth this accident and flood of fortune

12 So far exceed all instance, all discourse,
That I am ready to distrust mine eyes

14 And wrangle with my reason that persuades me
To any other trust but that I am mad,
Or else the lady's mad. Yet, if 'twere so,

17 She could not sway her house, command her followers,

18 Take and give back affairs and their dispatch
With such a smooth, discreet, and stable bearing
As I perceive she does. There's something in't

21 That is deceivable. But here the lady comes.
      Enter Olivia and Priest.

OLIVIA

Blame not this haste of mine. If you mean well,

IV, iii The house of Olivia **6** *was* had been; *credit* belief **12** *instance* example; *discourse* logic **14** *wrangle* dispute **17** *sway* rule **18** *dispatch* management **21** *deceivable* deceptive

Now go with me and with this holy man
Into the chantry by. There, before him,   24
And underneath that consecrated roof,
Plight me the full assurance of your faith,
That my most jealous and too doubtful soul   27
May live at peace. He shall conceal it
Whiles you are willing it shall come to note,   29
What time we will our celebration keep
According to my birth. What do you say?

SEBASTIAN

I'll follow this good man and go with you
And having sworn truth, ever will be true.

OLIVIA

Then lead the way, good father, and heavens so shine
That they may fairly note this act of mine.   *Exeunt.*

*

Enter Clown and Fabian.   V, i

FABIAN Now as thou lov'st me, let me see his letter.

CLOWN Good Master Fabian, grant me another request.

FABIAN Anything.

CLOWN Do not desire to see this letter.

FABIAN This is to give a dog, and in recompense desire
my dog again.

Enter Duke, Viola, Curio, and Lords.

DUKE Belong you to the Lady Olivia, friends?   7

CLOWN Ay, sir, we are some of her trappings.

DUKE I know thee well. How dost thou, my good fellow?

CLOWN Truly, sir, the better for my foes, and the worse
for my friends.

DUKE Just the contrary: the better for thy friends.

CLOWN No, sir, the worse.

DUKE How can that be?

CLOWN Marry, sir, they praise me and make an ass of me.

24 *chantry by* chapel near by   27 *jealous* anxious   29 *Whiles* until
V, i Before Olivia's house   7 *Belong you* i.e. are you in the service of

99

Now my foes tell me plainly I am an ass; so that by my
foes, sir, I profit in the knowledge of myself, and by my
18 friends I am abused; so that, conclusions to be as kisses,
if your four negatives make your two affirmatives, why
then, the worse for my friends, and the better for my
foes.

DUKE Why, this is excellent.

CLOWN By my troth, sir, no, though it please you to be
one of my friends.

DUKE Thou shalt not be the worse for me. There's gold.

25 CLOWN But that it would be double-dealing, sir, I would
you could make it another.

DUKE O, you give me ill counsel.

28 CLOWN Put your grace in your pocket, sir, for this once,
and let your flesh and blood obey it.

DUKE Well, I will be so much a sinner to be a double-
dealer. There's another.

32 CLOWN Primo, secundo, tertio is a good play; and the old
33 saying is 'The third pays for all.' The triplex, sir, is a
34 good tripping measure; or the bells of Saint Bennet, sir,
may put you in mind – one, two, three.

DUKE You can fool no more money out of me at this
37 throw. If you will let your lady know I am here to speak
with her, and bring her along with you, it may awake
my bounty further.

CLOWN Marry, sir, lullaby to your bounty till I come
again, I go, sir; but I would not have you to think that
my desire of having is the sin of covetousness. But, as
you say, sir, let your bounty take a nap; I will awake it
anon.   *Exit.*

Enter Antonio and Officers.

VIOLA
Here comes the man, sir, that did rescue me.

18 *abused* deceived   25 *double-dealing* (1) double giving, (2) deceit   28
your grace (1) title of address, (2) your generosity   32 *play* (probably a
children's game)   33 *triplex* triple time in music   34 *Saint Bennet* St
Benedict's church   37 *throw* throw of the dice

DUKE

That face of his I do remember well;
Yet when I saw it last, it was besmeared
As black as Vulcan in the smoke of war.   47
A baubling vessel was he captain of,   48
For shallow draught and bulk unprizable,   49
With which such scathful grapple did he make   50
With the most noble bottom of our fleet   51
That very envy and the tongue of loss   52
Cried fame and honor on him. What's the matter?

I. OFFICER

Orsino, this is that Antonio
That took the Phoenix and her fraught from Candy;   55
And this is he that did the Tiger board
When your young nephew Titus lost his leg.
Here in the streets, desperate of shame and state,   58
In private brabble did we apprehend him.   59

VIOLA

He did me kindness, sir; drew on my side;
But in conclusion put strange speech upon me.
I know not what 'twas but distraction.   62

DUKE

Notable pirate, thou salt-water thief,
What foolish boldness brought thee to their mercies
Whom thou in terms so bloody and so dear   65
Hast made thine enemies?

ANTONIO   Orsino, noble sir,
Be pleased that I shake off these names you give me.
Antonio never yet was thief or pirate,
Though I confess, on base and ground enough,   69
Orsino's enemy. A witchcraft drew me hither.
That most ingrateful boy there by your side

---

47 *Vulcan* Roman god of fire and patron of metal workers   48 *baubling*
trifling   49 *unprizable* unworthy of being taken as a prize   50 *scathful*
harmful   51 *bottom* ship   52 *very envy* even malice; *loss* the losers   55
fraught cargo; *Candy* Candia, Crete   58 *desperate* reckless   59 *brabble*
brawl   62 *distraction* madness   65 *dear* costly   69 *base and ground* solid
grounds

From the rude sea's enragèd and foamy mouth
Did I redeem. A wrack past hope he was.
His life I gave him, and did thereto add
My love without retention or restraint,
All his in dedication. For his sake
77 Did I expose myself (pure for his love)
Into the danger of this adverse town;
Drew to defend him when he was beset;
Where being apprehended, his false cunning
(Not meaning to partake with me in danger)
82 Taught him to face me out of his acquaintance,
83 And grew a twenty years removèd thing
While one would wink; denied me mine own purse,
85 Which I had recommended to his use
Not half an hour before.

VIOLA   How can this be?

DUKE
When came he to this town?

ANTONIO
To-day, my lord; and for three months before,
No int'rim, not a minute's vacancy,
Both day and night did we keep company.

Enter Olivia and Attendants.

DUKE
Here comes the Countess; now heaven walks on earth.
But for thee, fellow: fellow, thy words are madness.
Three months this youth hath tended upon me;
But more of that anon. Take him aside.

OLIVIA
95 What would my lord, but that he may not have,
Wherein Olivia may seem serviceable?
Cesario, you do not keep promise with me.

VIOLA
Madam?

---

77 *pure* purely   82 *face . . . acquaintance* pretend not to know me   83
removèd estranged   85 *recommended* entrusted   95 *but that* except what

DUKE
Gracious Olivia –
OLIVIA
What do you say, Cesario ? – Good my lord –
VIOLA
My lord would speak ; my duty hushes me.
OLIVIA
If it be aught to the old tune, my lord,
It is as fat and fulsome to mine ear   103
As howling after music.
DUKE   Still so cruel ?
OLIVIA
Still so constant, lord.
DUKE
What, to perverseness ? You uncivil lady,
To whose ingrate and unauspicious altars
My soul the faithfull'st off'rings have breathed out
That e'er devotion tendered. What shall I do ?
OLIVIA
Even what it please my lord, that shall become him.
DUKE
Why should I not, had I the heart to do it,
Like to th' Egyptian thief at point of death,   112
Kill what I love ? (A savage jealousy
That sometime savors nobly.) But hear me this :
Since you to non-regardance cast my faith,   115
And that I partly know the instrument
That screws me from my true place in your favor,   117
Live you the marble-breasted tyrant still.
But this your minion, whom I know you love,   119
And whom, by heaven I swear, I tender dearly,   120
Him will I tear out of that cruel eye
Where he sits crownèd in his master's spite.   122

103 *fat* superfluous; *fulsome* offensive 112 *th' Egyptian thief* Thyamis in the *Aethiopica* by Heliodorus 115 *non-regardance* neglect 117 *screws* pries 119 *minion* favorite 120 *tender* hold 122 *in . . . spite* despite his master

Come, boy, with me. My thoughts are ripe in mischief.
I'll sacrifice the lamb that I do love
To spite a raven's heart within a dove.   *[Going.]*

VIOLA

126 And I, most jocund, apt, and willingly,
127 To do you rest a thousand deaths would die. *[Following.]*

OLIVIA

Where goes Cesario?

VIOLA   After him I love
More than I love these eyes, more than my life,
130 More, by all mores, than e'er I shall love wife.
If I do feign, you witnesses above
Punish my life for tainting of my love!

OLIVIA

Ay me detested! how am I beguiled!

VIOLA

Who does beguile you? Who does do you wrong?

OLIVIA

Hast thou forgot thyself? Is it so long?
Call forth the holy father.   *[Exit an Attendant.]*

DUKE *[to Viola]*   Come, away!

OLIVIA

Whither, my lord? Cesario, husband, stay.

DUKE

Husband?

OLIVIA   Ay, husband. Can he that deny?

DUKE

Her husband, sirrah?

VIOLA   No, my lord, not I.

OLIVIA

Alas, it is the baseness of thy fear
141 That makes thee strangle thy propriety.
Fear not, Cesario; take thy fortunes up;
Be that thou know'st thou art, and then thou art

---

126 *apt* properly   **127** *do you rest* give you peace   **130** *all mores* i.e. all
conceivable comparisons   **141** *propriety* identity

As great as that thou fear'st.   144
    Enter Priest.
                    O, welcome, father!
Father, I charge thee by thy reverence
Here to unfold – though lately we intended
To keep in darkness what occasion now
Reveals before 'tis ripe – what thou dost know
Hath newly passed between this youth and me.

PRIEST
A contract of eternal bond of love,
Confirmed by mutual joinder of your hands,
Attested by the holy close of lips,   152
Strength'ned by interchangement of your rings;
And all the ceremony of this compact
Sealed in my function, by my testimony;
Since when, my watch hath told me, toward my grave
I have travelled but two hours.

DUKE
O thou dissembling cub, what wilt thou be
When time hath sowed a grizzle on thy case?   159
Or will not else thy craft so quickly grow
That thine own trip shall be thine overthrow?   161
Farewell, and take her; but direct thy feet
Where thou and I, henceforth, may never meet.

VIOLA
My lord, I do protest.

OLIVIA   O, do not swear.
Hold little faith, though thou hast too much fear.   165
    Enter Sir Andrew.

ANDREW For the love of God, a surgeon! Send one pres-   166
  ently to Sir Toby.

OLIVIA What's the matter?

ANDREW Has broke my head across, and has given Sir   169

---

144 *that thou fear'st* i.e. the Duke 152 *close* meeting 159 *a grizzle* grey
hair; *case* sheath, i.e. skin 161 *trip* trickery 165 *little* a little 166
presently at once 169 *Has* he has

Toby a bloody coxcomb too. For the love of God,
your help! I had rather than forty pounds I were at
home.

OLIVIA Who has done this, Sir Andrew?

ANDREW The Count's gentleman, one Cesario. We took
174   him for a coward, but he's the very devil incardinate.

DUKE My gentleman Cesario?

176 ANDREW Od's lifelings, here he is! You broke my head
for nothing; and that that I did, I was set on to do't by
Sir Toby.

VIOLA
Why do you speak to me? I never hurt you.
You drew your sword upon me without cause,
But I bespake you fair and hurt you not.
    Enter [Sir] Toby and Clown.

ANDREW If a bloody coxcomb be a hurt, you have hurt
me. I think you set nothing by a bloody coxcomb. Here
184   comes Sir Toby halting; you shall hear more. But if he
185   had not been in drink, he would have tickled you othergates than he did.

DUKE How now, gentleman? How is't with you?

TOBY That's all one! Has hurt me, and there's th' end
on't. Sot, didst see Dick Surgeon, sot?

CLOWN O, he's drunk, Sir Toby, an hour agone. His eyes
191   were set at eight i' th' morning.

192 TOBY Then he's a rogue and a passy measures pavin. I
hate a drunken rogue.

OLIVIA Away with him! Who hath made this havoc with
them?

ANDREW I'll help you, Sir Toby, because we'll be dressed
together.

TOBY Will you help? An ass-head and a coxcomb and a
knave, a thin-faced knave, a gull?

---

174 *incardinate* incarnate 176 *Od's lifelings* by God's little life 184
halting limping 185 *othergates* otherwise 191 *set* fixed or gone down, i.e.
closed 192 *passy measures pavin* an eight-bar double-slow dance

OLIVIA Get him to bed, and let his hurt be looked to.
    [Exeunt Clown, Fabian, Sir Toby, and Sir Andrew.]
    Enter Sebastian.

SEBASTIAN
  I am sorry, madam, I have hurt your kinsman;
  But had it been the brother of my blood,
  I must have done no less with wit and safety.   203
  You throw a strange regard upon me, and by that   204
  I do perceive it hath offended you.
  Pardon me, sweet one, even for the vows
  We made each other but so late ago.

DUKE
  One face, one voice, one habit, and two persons –   208
  A natural perspective that is and is not.   209

SEBASTIAN
  Antonio, O my dear Antonio,
  How have the hours racked and tortured me
  Since I have lost thee!

ANTONIO
  Sebastian are you?

SEBASTIAN   Fear'st thou that, Antonio?

ANTONIO
  How have you made division of yourself?
  An apple cleft in two is not more twin
  Than these two creatures. Which is Sebastian?

OLIVIA
  Most wonderful.

SEBASTIAN
  Do I stand there? I never had a brother;
  Nor can there be that deity in my nature
  Of here and everywhere. I had a sister,
  Whom the blind waves and surges have devoured.
  Of charity, what kin are you to me?
  What countryman? What name? What parentage?

---

203 *wit and safety* intelligent regard for my safety **204** *strange regard*
estranged look **208** *habit* dress **209** *perspective* glass producing an optical
illusion

VIOLA

Of Messaline ; Sebastian was my father ;
Such a Sebastian was my brother too ;
226　So went he suited to his watery tomb.
If spirits can assume both form and suit,
You come to fright us.

SEBASTIAN　　　　　　A spirit I am indeed,
229　But am in that dimension grossly clad
230　Which from the womb I did participate.
231　Were you a woman, as the rest goes even,
I should my tears let fall upon your cheek
And say, 'Thrice welcome, drownèd Viola !'

VIOLA

My father had a mole upon his brow.

SEBASTIAN

And so had mine.

VIOLA

And died that day when Viola from her birth
Had numb'red thirteen years.

SEBASTIAN

238　O, that record is lively in my soul !
He finishèd indeed his mortal act
That day that made my sister thirteen years.

VIOLA

241　If nothing lets to make us happy both
But this my masculine usurped attire,
Do not embrace me till each circumstance
244　Of place, time, fortune do cohere and jump
That I am Viola ; which to confirm,
I'll bring you to a captain in this town,
247　Where lie my maiden weeds ; by whose gentle help
I was preserved to serve this noble Count.
All the occurrence of my fortune since

226 *suited* dressed　229 *dimension* form ; *grossly* in the flesh　230 *participate*
inherit　231 *rest goes even* other circumstances allow　238 *record* memory
241 *lets* hinders　244 *jump* agree completely　247 *weeds* clothes

Hath been between this lady and this lord.

SEBASTIAN *[to Olivia]*
So comes it, lady, you have been mistook.
But nature to her bias drew in that.   252
You would have been contracted to a maid ;
Nor are you therein, by my life, deceived :
You are betrothed both to a maid and man.

DUKE
Be not amazed ; right noble is his blood.
If this be so, as yet the glass seems true,   257
I shall have share in this most happy wrack.
      [To Viola]
Boy, thou hast said to me a thousand times
Thou never shouldst love woman like to me.

VIOLA
And all those sayings will I over swear,   261
And all those swearings keep as true in soul
As doth that orbèd continent the fire   263
That severs day from night.

DUKE   Give me thy hand,
And let me see thee in thy woman's weeds.

VIOLA
The captain that did bring me first on shore
Hath my maid's garments. He upon some action   267
Is now in durance, at Malvolio's suit,
A gentleman, and follower of my lady's.

OLIVIA
He shall enlarge him. Fetch Malvolio hither.   270
And yet alas, now I remember me,
They say, poor gentleman, he's much distract.
      Enter Clown with a letter, and Fabian.
A most extracting frenzy of mine own   273

---

252 *to her bias drew* i.e. drew you into a natural course   **257** *glass* perspective glass   **261** *over swear* swear over again   **263** *orbèd continent* sphere of the sun   **267** *action* legal charge   **270** *enlarge* free   **273** *extracting* distracting

From my remembrance clearly banished his.
How does he, sirrah?

276 CLOWN Truly, madam, he holds Belzebub at the stave's
end as well as a man in his case may do. Has here writ a
letter to you; I should have given't you to-day morning.
279 But as a madman's epistles are no gospels, so it skills not
much when they are delivered.

OLIVIA Open't and read it.

282 CLOWN Look then to be well edified, when the fool delivers the madman. [Reads in a loud voice] 'By the Lord,
madam' –

OLIVIA How now? Art thou mad?

CLOWN No, madam, I do but read madness. An your lady-
287 ship will have it as it ought to be, you must allow vox.

OLIVIA Prithee read i' thy right wits.

CLOWN So I do, madonna; but to read his right wits is to
290 read thus. Therefore perpend, my princess, and give ear.

OLIVIA [to Fabian] Read it you, sirrah.

FABIAN (reads) 'By the Lord, madam, you wrong me,
and the world shall know it. Though you have put me
into darkness, and given your drunken cousin rule over
me, yet have I the benefit of my senses as well as your
ladyship. I have your own letter that induced me to the
semblance I put on; with the which I doubt not but to
do myself much right, or you much shame. Think of me
as you please. I leave my duty a little unthought of,
and speak out of my injury.

'The madly used Malvolio.'

OLIVIA Did he write this?

CLOWN Ay, madam.

DUKE This savors not much of distraction.

OLIVIA
See him delivered, Fabian; bring him hither.

[Exit Fabian.]

***

276–77 holds . . . end i.e. holds the devil off   279 skills matters   282
delivers speaks the words of   287 vox voice-volume   290 perpend consider

My lord, so please you, these things further thought on,
To think me as well a sister as a wife,
One day shall crown th' alliance on't, so please you,
Here at my house and at my proper cost.   309

DUKE
Madam, I am most apt t' embrace your offer.   310
   [To Viola]
Your master quits you; and for your service done him,   311
So much against the mettle of your sex,
So far beneath your soft and tender breeding,
And since you called me master for so long,
Here is my hand; you shall from this time be
Your master's mistress.

OLIVIA   A sister; you are she.
   Enter [Fabian, with] Malvolio.

DUKE
Is this the madman?

OLIVIA   Ay, my lord, this same.
How now, Malvolio?

MALVOLIO   Madam, you have done me wrong,
Notorious wrong.

OLIVIA   Have I, Malvolio? No.

MALVOLIO
Lady, you have. Pray you peruse that letter.
You must not now deny it is your hand.
Write from it if you can, in hand or phrase,   322
Or say 'tis not your seal, not your invention.   323
You can say none of this. Well, grant it then,
And tell me, in the modesty of honor,   325
Why you have given me such clear lights of favor,
Bade me come smiling and cross-gartered to you,
To put on yellow stockings, and to frown
Upon Sir Toby and the lighter people;   329

---

309 *proper* own   **310** *apt* ready   **311** *quits* releases   **322** *from it* differently
323 *invention* composition   **325** *in . . . honor* with honorable propriety
329 *lighter* lesser

And, acting this in an obedient hope,
Why have you suffered me to be imprisoned,
Kept in a dark house, visited by the priest,
333 And made the most notorious geck and gull
That e'er invention played on? Tell me why.

OLIVIA

Alas, Malvolio, this is not my writing,
Though I confess much like the character;
But, out of question, 'tis Maria's hand.
And now I do bethink me, it was she
First told me thou wast mad. Thou cam'st in smiling,
340 And in such forms which here were presupposed
Upon thee in the letter. Prithee be content.
342 This practice hath most shrewdly passed upon thee;
But when we know the grounds and authors of it,
Thou shalt be both the plaintiff and the judge
Of thine own cause.

FABIAN   Good madam, here me speak,
And let no quarrel, nor no brawl to come,
Taint the condition of this present hour,
Which I have wond'red at. In hope it shall not,
Most freely I confess myself and Toby
Set this device against Malvolio here,
351 Upon some stubborn and uncourteous parts
We had conceived against him. Maria writ
353 The letter, at Sir Toby's great importance,
In recompense whereof he hath married her.
How with a sportful malice it was followed
May rather pluck on laughter than revenge,
If that the injuries be justly weighed
That have on both sides passed.

OLIVIA

359 Alas, poor fool, how have they baffled thee!

---

333 *geck and gull* ludicrous dupe   340–41 *presupposed Upon thee* put upon you beforehand   342 *shrewdly passed* maliciously been put   351 *Upon* on account of   353 *importance* importunity   359 *baffled thee* disgraced you publicly

CLOWN Why, 'some are born great, some achieve greatness, and some have greatness thrown upon them.' I
was one, sir, in this interlude, one Sir Topas, sir; but   362
that's all one. 'By the Lord, fool, I am not mad!' But do
you remember, 'Madam, why laugh you at such a
barren rascal? An you smile not, he's gagged'? And
thus the whirligig of time brings in his revenges.

MALVOLIO I'll be revenged on the whole pack of you!
                                             [Exit.]

OLIVIA
  He hath been most notoriously abused.

DUKE
  Pursue him and entreat him to a peace.
  He hath not told us of the captain yet.
  When that is known, and golden time convents,   371
  A solemn combination shall be made
  Of our dear souls. Meantime, sweet sister,
  We will not part from hence. Cesario, come –
  For so you shall be while you are a man,
  But when in other habits you are seen,
  Orsino's mistress and his fancy's queen.   377
                          Exeunt [all but the Clown].

                    Clown sings.

    When that I was and a little tiny boy,
        With hey, ho, the wind and the rain,
    A foolish thing was but a toy,
        For the rain it raineth every day.

    But when I came to man's estate,
        With hey, ho, the wind and the rain,
    'Gainst knaves and thieves men shut their gate,
        For the rain it raineth every day.

---

362 *interlude* an early form of dramatic entertainment 371 *convents* is
convenient 377 *fancy's* love's

But when I came, alas, to wive,
   With hey, ho, the wind and the rain,
By swaggering could I never thrive,
   For the rain it raineth every day.

390   But when I came unto my beds,
   With hey, ho, the wind and the rain,
With tosspots still had drunken heads,
   For the rain it raineth every day.

A great while ago the world begun,
   With hey, ho, the wind and the rain;
But that's all one, our play is done,
   And we'll strive to please you every day.   *[Exit.]*

A selection of books published by Penguin is listed on the following pages.

For a complete list of books available from Penguin in the United States, write to Dept. DG, Penguin Books, 299 Murray Hill Parkway, East Rutherford, New Jersey 07073.

For a complete list of books available from Penguin in Canada, write to Penguin Books Canada Limited, 2801 John Street, Markham, Ontario L3R 1B4.

The Complete Pelican
SHAKESPEARE

To fill the need for a convenient and authoritative one-volume edition, the thirty-eight books in the Pelican series have been brought together.

THE COMPLETE PELICAN SHAKESPEARE includes all the material contained in the separate volumes, together with a 50,000-word General Introduction and full bibliographies. It contains the first nineteen pages of the First Folio in reduced facsimile, five new drawings, and illustrated endpapers. 9¾ × 7³⁄₁₆ inches, 1520 pages.

THE AGE OF
SHAKESPEARE

Edited by Boris Ford

This second volume of *The Pelican Guide to English Literature* covers the Elizabethan literary renaissance. An extensive survey of Elizabethan literature and society is followed by a number of essays that consider in detail the work and importance of dramatists, poets, and prose writers—Cyril Tourneur, George Chapman, Thomas Middleton, Samuel Daniel, Sir Walter Ralegh, and Francis Bacon, among many others. The emphasis is on the dramatists, and five of the essays are devoted to Shakespeare's plays alone. An appendix gives short biographies of authors and lists critical commentaries, books for further study and reference, and standard editions of Elizabethan works. Boris Ford is Professor of Education and Dean of the School of Cultural and Community Studies at the University of Sussex, England.

INTRODUCING SHAKESPEARE
Third Edition

G. B. Harrison

Now a classic, this volume has been the best popular introduction to Shakespeare for over thirty years. Dr. G. B. Harrison discusses first Shakespeare's legend and then his tantalizingly ill-recorded life. Harrison describes the Elizabethan playhouse (with the help of a set of graphic reconstructions) and examines the effect of its complicated structure on the plays themselves. It is in the chapter on the Lord Chamberlain's Players that Shakespeare and his associates are most clearly seen against their background of theatrical rivalry, literary piracy, the closing of the playhouses because of the plague, the famous performance of *Richard II* in support of the Earl of Essex, and the fire that finally destroyed the Globe Theater.

SHAKESPEARE

Anthony Burgess

Bare entries in parish registers, a document or two, and a few legends and contemporary references make up the known life of William Shakespeare. Anthony Burgess has clothed these attractively with an extensive knowledge of Elizabethan and Jacobean England for this elaborately illustrated biography. The characters of the men Shakespeare knew, the influence of his life on his plays, and the stirring events that must have been in the minds of author, actors, and audience are engagingly described here by a writer who sees "Will" not as an ethereal bard but as a sensitive, sensual, and shrewd man from the provinces who turned his art to fortune in the most exciting years of England's history. "It was a touch of near genius to choose Mr. Burgess to write the text for a richly illustrated life of Shakespeare, for his wonderfully well-stocked mind and essentially wayward spirit are just right for summoning up an apparition of the bard which is more convincing than most"—David Holloway, *London Daily Telegraph*. With 48 plates in color and nearly 100 black-and-white illustrations.